The Five

Lesbian Brothers'

Guide to Life

THE

FIVE
LESBIAN
BROTHERS'

GUIDE TO LIFE

A Collection of Helpful Hints
and Fabricated Facts for
Today's Gay Girl

ILLUSTRATED BY DONNA EVANS

A FIRESIDE BOOK
Published by Simon & Schuster

Fireside
Rockefeller Center
1230 Avenue of the Americas
New York, NY 10020
Copyright © 1997 by The Five Lesbian Brothers

Illustrations © 1997 by Donna Evans
Additional illustrations by Dominique Dibbell

Manufactured in the United States of America

1 3 5 7 9 10 8 6 4 2

Library of Congress Cataloging-in-Publication Data
Five Lesbian Brothers (Theater troupe)
The Five Lesbian Brothers' guide to life :
a collection of helpful hints and fabricated facts for today's gay girl /
illustrated by Donna Evans
p.   cm.
"A Fireside book."
1. Lesbians—Humor.   2. Lesbians.   I. Title.   II. Title:
5 Lesbian Brothers' guide to life.   III. Title: Guide to life.
PN6231.L43F58   1997   97-25996
818'.540208—DC21   CIP
ISBN 0-684-81384-X

Acknowledgments

We would like to thank our editor, Betsy Radin Herman, without whom this project would not have been possible, and our agent Stephen Pevner, who made it all happen. Thanks! We also owe a debt of gratitude to the following people who gave their time, resources, and insights to us throughout the process: Sama Blackwell, Marlene Besterman, Betsy Farrell, Stephanie Nye, Susan Finque, Madeleine Olnek, Dan Hurlin and the Hangar Studio, New York Theatre Workshop, DYKE TV, Lambda Legal Defense, Linda Heidinger, Nancy Blaine and Rebecca Cole, Cara Palladino and Laurie Arbeiter, Libby Smith, Tom Keith, Hillary Carlip, Ed Corley, Phranc, Maggie Garb, Gretchen Phillips, Consuelo Gonzales, Susan Murray, Lisa Horowitz and Anne Gibeau, Nora Burns, Terence Michael, Janet Clark and Ellen Bone, John Hoffman, Pat Power, and all of our friends and family who listened during our creative process. Thank you all so much for your generous support of the Brothers!

The Brothers dedicate this book lovingly
to all of the women at the WOW Cafe in New York City,
where we got our degrees in Lesbotology.

Contents

Preface

So Who the Hell Are the Five Lesbian Brothers, Anyway?

We are five gals from New York City who are normally a theater troupe, but in this case, we are authors. In our seven years together, we have toured across the country, meeting many a fine lesbian along the way. Because of our extensive mingling with the dykes of America, we were recruited by Simon & Schuster to write this book. We found it interesting that WE were in the position of being recruited by STRAIGHT people, since we are usually accused of doing that ourselves. Anyway, in spite of the contradictory nature of our name, we want to be clear that all five of us are actual card-carrying lesbians. Sometimes, people think that we are really brothers or that we are wacky gay men or that we are transsexuals, and sometimes they still think that after they meet us.

We would like to assure you from the outset that we are indeed fully certified 100 percent grade-A lesbians.

And Just What Exactly Is This Book About?

This is a humor book, a reference book, a self-help book, and a political tome. It is an ill-researched but lovingly prepared primer that is chock-full of absolute truths and fabricated facts, often indistinguishable from one another. It is written with you in mind, whether you are a baby dyke, an old amazon, or just a friendly lesbophile. You can use this book to make yourself laugh, to make your friends laugh, to upset your parents, to educate the uninformed, or as a coming-out tool. Just leave it on your desk at work! You'll find all those pesky questions about your boyfriend will dry right up! Of course, our hope is that, as with any humor book, you will keep our book in the bathroom. We believe if you can be out and proud while sitting on the toilet, you can be out and proud anywhere. Enjoy!

The Five
Lesbian Brothers'
Guide to Life

PART I

DEFINING
OUR(LESBIAN)SELVES

The "Dyketionary"
(Abridged)

R emember the first time you heard the word *lesbian?* For most of us, that first time is etched on our minds. It was like hearing about Disneyland and thinking, "That sounds like fun! How can I get there?" "Just what is a lesbian?" you thought. It was only logical that you would seek definition. So you started, of course, with the dictionary, only to find a nebulous and baffling definition such as this one:

(1) lez be en adj. 1. of or relating to Lesbos; 2. [fr. the reputed homosexual band associated with Sappho of Lesbos; of or relating to homosexuality between females.]

This definition doesn't tell you much except that Sappho was the first lesbian to have a band.

Sooner or later, the smart lesbian realizes she must define herself. We have spoken to hundreds of women about their self-identification process and this is what they told us:

"I am a lesbian because I have sexual feelings and primary emotional attachments for women. Mostly."

Carolanne, age forty-two

"I'm a lesbian because I'm too lazy to shave my legs."

Lourdes, age twenty-four

"I am a lesbian because I have made a political choice to play into the capitalist death machine as little as possible. Women just love life more than profit."

Wanda, age fifty

"I am a lesbian because I can't help it."

Shirley, age sixty-nine

"It's all about smell."

Lettie, age fifty-five

"I'm not really a career lesbian. I am just in love with Margaret for the time being."

Shanequa, age thirty-one

"I am a lesbian because heterosexuality was too boring for me."

Leslie, age seventeen

"I became a lesbian because I hate my parents and I wanted to try and ruin their lives."

Mai, age twenty-one

The more lesbians you talk to, the more you realize that no two lesbians are alike. We come from every walk, crawl, skip, limp, and roll of life. You find yourself wondering, "Is there any single unifying characteristic? Is there any one thing you can point to and say, 'This is it. This is the thing that *all* lesbians have in common'?"

Well, you can rest easy now because the Five Lesbian Brothers have identified the ONE TRAIT that is shared by ALL LESBIANS:

ALL LESBIANS WEAR COMFORTABLE CLOTHING

Sure, some lesbians may look more stylish than others, but though it might *look* like a pump, it will always *feel* like a sneaker.

The Twelve Basic Types of Lesbians

Although lesbians cross all geographic, cultural, religious, economic, and racial borders, we here at the Five Lesbian Brothers Wind Tunnel and Test Kitchens have identified the Twelve Basic Types of Lesbians. No matter what your background, you're sure to see yourself in one or more of these categories. In no particular order, they are:

One: The Butch

The Butch is a woman who is comfortable with her thumbs hitched in the belt loops of her 501s. (Variations include: Stone Butch, Butch Bottom, Femmy Butch, and Matt Dillon.)

Two: The Femme

The Femme is a woman whose earthquake-survival kit includes a lipstick. (Variations include: Ultra Femme, Butchy Femme, Femme Top, Charles Nelson Reilly.)

Three: The Tomboy

The Tomboy is that young-
ster who seems to always
know where the fuse box is
and how to get the lawn
mower going. Unafraid of
physical work, especially if
it involves power tools, this

budding female homo can be seen hanging out with others like her in tragically small, ostracized groups in
parking lots, dressed like boys of her same age group.
This gal is on the top of the batting order for softball and
thinks it's cool to remove the dead mouse from behind
the chemical cabinet in science class.

Four: The Lesbian Parent

These women are part of the lesbian baby boom, that
statistical category that never enters into the govern-
ment's census of single-parent households run by
women. Thanks to ever-increasing access to fertility

technology, many of these women got
pregnant practically on their own
with no pesky ex-husband hanging
around making threats. As a result,
more lesbian moms are out and
proudly serving the tofu-spelt puffs
at the PTA potluck.

Five: The Diesel Dyke

She is the kind of lesbian who could not possibly be mistaken for a straight woman, although in some rural parts of the country these women actually are straight. Characterized by their heavily male-identified wardrobe choices, these women are most comfortable driving heavy machinery while intoxicated. A dangerous occupational hazard, yes, but they are part of our community, too.

SIx: The Jock

The Jock has prominent deltoids (a result of twenty years of daily gym workouts) and at least one serious scar from knee or elbow surgery. She probably was a member of an Olympic team or was in the Olympic trials or at least watches the Olympics fanatically. The Jock thinks of her black sweats as formal wear.

Seven: The Lesbian Professional

You've seen her and probably didn't even know it. She's stylish and wealthy and probably lives in a major urban hub. She is a powerful corporate head, company manager, attorney, or stockbroker. This lesbian dresses for success in a very chic, androgynous *comme des garçons* style. She's not afraid to take up  space at a board meeting or shout down the guy who shorted her in the deli. Though she probably doesn't have time to volunteer for a lesbian hotline, she'll be happy to show her support by writing a check.

Eight: The Professional Lesbian

 The Professional Lesbian does not have a full-time job. Her wardrobe of overalls and leather jacket covered with buttons like "Keep your laws off my hot, wet, lesbian pussy" renders her largely unemployable by the mainstream, although she makes do with a variety of part-time jobs, such as bouncer at the Clit Club and tarot card reader. She lives in the homes of various lovers and friends and moves around a lot.

Nine: The Avenging Lesbian (Activist)

This lesbian looks a little like the Professional Lesbian, but she has a more focused gleam in her eye and she knows how to clean herself up for an appearance on a talk show. She is the warrior for us all who makes herself known to the world at large through the purposeful antics she employs to disrupt the status quo. The Avenging Lesbian's mind is always working on ways to turn even a simple trip to the grocery store into a stand for equal rights, and that's why she's fun on a date (if you don't mind spending your first night together in jail).

Ten: The Separatist

If you're a woman, you don't see this gal much. If you're a fella, she's as elusive as Big Foot. Living out in Womyn's Land and associating only with her own sex, the "Sep" is the Lubavitcher of the lesbian community. In the Separatist household, menstrual prints adorn the walls and the cupboards are animal-product free. Boy children are sent to live with their bio-dads and all music is acoustic and female-generated. Extreme, yes, but they are the standard-bearers for us all, making our simple hatred of men seem reasonable.

Eleven: The Lesbian Who Sleeps with Men (formerly "the Bisexual")

You didn't see these girls so much back in the old days before "Queer Unity." It used to be the "Gay" Pride March, then they added on lesbians, then bisexuals, then transsexuals, then Sophie B. Hawkins. But now the lesbian who sleeps with men is an accepted member of our community. She is proud to be a lesbian and take the rap for it, but every once in a while she gets a hankering for a taste of the big salami. She might have a boyfriend for years but will continue to call herself a lesbian, claiming she is "just going through a phase."

Twelve: The Slave/Master

If a lesbian wants to be tied up and another lesbian agrees to do it, they have participated in a master/slave exchange. The first gal is the master for demanding to be treated like a slave. The second gal ties her up and acts

like a master, saying things like "I
will not give you the dildo, not
today," and in real life the master
does everything the slave wants.
Any questions?

Thirteen: The Closet Case

Straight people are often com-
pletely oblivious to the telltale signs of the
closet case, but if you are a gay or a lesbian
yourself, detecting the secret sapphite is a
snap. Just see who walks away from the conversation when you start to talk about
spousal equivalency. Yup, she's the one who
looks all panicky during same-sex embraces
and changes her clothes in a bathroom stall
after a strenuous gym workout, forgoing the showers
entirely. She'll add awkward feminine touches to her
wardrobe and still look like a longshoreman in a peach
dress in your wedding party. Her "date" is always an
incredibly handsome, well-groomed fellow who takes a
special interest in your interior design challenges. You
may want to make friends with this lost lamb, but be
careful—she's the type who'll get you thrown out of the
military quicker than you can say "J. Edgar Hoover."

TOP-TEN LESBIAN PROFESSIONS

1. Social worker
2. Firefighter
3. Librarian
4. Fashion model
5. Gynecologist

6. Nun
7. Prison warden
8. Predatory gym teacher
9. Olympic gold medalist
10. Attorney general

The Butch/Femme Controversy

Are you butch or femme? Or are you just offended by this question? We lesbians have a good time playing masculine/feminine roles. Are we playing, or is there something to this butch/femme "dykeotomy" that is inherent in our nature? Find out where you fall on the spectrum by taking the following test.

Butch/Femme Quiz

1. When you saw Linda Hamilton in <u>Terminator 2</u>, you wanted to:

   ❏ a. Be her.
   ❏ b. Be her love slave.

2. You know it's time to do your laundry when:

   ❏ a. Your favorite blouse is dirty.
   ❏ b. Your last pair of BVDs is dirty.

3. You like to spend your Thanksgiving holiday:

   ❏ a. Watching people enjoy your cranberry/apple pie, which you made from scratch.
   ❏ b. Watching the Redskins defeat the Cowboys.

4. You and your mother always fought during the holidays because she didn't want you to go to your aunt's house wearing:

   ❏ a. Pants.
   ❏ b. Hotpants.

5. You are certain that pantyhose are a tool of the patriarchy because:

    ❏ a. You feel physically ill when you put them on.
    ❏ b. You know run-resistant pantyhose exist but they won't sell them to the public!

Look below for your amazing results:

Amazing Results (#1): Oh, come on! We can't believe you actually took this quiz! Butch/Femme! Nobody really believes these tired old patriarchal stereotypes anymore, do they?

Amazing Results (#2): Okay, okay, if you chose *B* for every answer, regardless of what the sentence said, simply because you thought the letter *B* stood for "Butch," then you are definitely a Butch.

The Lesbian Tongue
(Glossary of Lesbian Words and Phrases)

Do you speak Lesbian? We don't exactly have our own language, but there are certain words and phrases we endow with our own special meaning. In this glossary, the first definition (1) gives the "standard definition" and the second (2) signifies the "lesbian meaning."

Affair—1. *n.* a social event, often catered. **2.** *n.* a lover who is not your girlfriend, often catered to.

Animal companion—1. *n.* a friend for your pet. **2.** *n.* a pet who is your friend.

Bottom—1. *n.* endearing name for the buttocks. **2.** *n.* the passive partner during S/M sexual union.

Breeder—1. *n.* an animal put out to stud. **2.** *n.* heterosexual male or female.

Breeder trophy—1. *n.* a prize given for good breeding. **2.** *n.* the child of a straight couple.

Butch—1. *n.* nickname for your butcher. 2. *n.* mannish lesbian.

Commitment—1. *n.* the act of committing; the state of being committed. 2. *n.* a second date.

Ex-lover—1. *n.* a person who used to be your lover. 2. *n.* your best friend's new lover.

Fisting—1. *v.* to have or get involved in a fight. 2. *v.* to have or get involved in sex. **As in:** *When your new girlfriend asks how big your hands are, it doesn't necessarily mean you are getting gloves for Christmas.*

Gender—1. *adj.* boy or girl. 2. restrictive labels assigned at birth to encourage conformity and control the populace.

Gender bender—1. *n.* a mixture of masculine and feminine traits. 2. what happens when a Butch goes to the ladies' room at the mall.

Humus—1. *n.* rich, fertile soil. 2. *n.* snack-food paste made from puréed chickpeas, garlic, tahini, cumin, and a little lemon.

Pet—1. *n.* a domesticated animal. 2. *n.* what a lesbian calls her lover.

Process—1. *n.* Any sequential set of actions that results in the desired goal. 2. *v.* To continually go over the same emotional ground with a partner.

Program—1. *n.* a television show. 2. *n.* a twelve-step group (i.e., AA, ACOA, NA, DA). **As in:** *When the woman you just met at the community center says she is in a "program," it doesn't mean that you should look for her on Saturday night, Channel 4, at 8:00 P.M.*

Pussy—1. *n.* a synonym for cat. 2. *n.* synonym for cat. **As in:** *It's no secret that a lesbian's best friend is the furry little creature that lives in her lap.*

Relationship—1. *n.* a state of relating. 2. *n.* a state of no more sex. *(See lesbian bed death, below.)*

Snap-on—1. *n.* line of tools advertised by half-naked girls.

Strap-on—*n.* tool worn by your half-naked girlfriend.

Therapy—1. *n.* psychological treatment designed to help one overcome emotional problems. **2.** *n.* the most popular lesbian pastime after softball.

Top—1. *n.* a short-sleeved or sleeveless shirt or blouse. **2.** *n.* the controlling partner during S/M sexual union.

Lesbian Phraseology
A Sampling

Butch in the streets/Femme in the sheets

As any consumer in our society can tell you, when you get your purchase home from the showroom, it sometimes doesn't look the same as it did in the store. The same holds true for those butchier-than-thou girls found at almost any dyke gathering. This phrase denotes that oh-so top girl who, once in the privacy of your bedroom, cries and squeals for you to do her first.

Full-on homo

This is a woman who "never really thought about sleeping with a woman before" but can be awakened into Kinsey 6 homosexuality when the right conditions are present. Talk to her in a civilized tone about the fluidity of sexuality and she will sound reserved and act interested only on an intellectual plane. But get her naked in a hot tub with a hit of Herbal Ecstasy and she'll be wondering why she didn't act on her feelings ten years ago while she plows your south forty.

Lesbian bed death

An affliction of long-term lesbian couples who share everything except sex; characterized by heavy television watching, reluctance to stay up after midnight, and a crusty bottle of lube rotting away in a closet.

Lesbian chic

Phenomenon of media attention focused on well-dressed lesbians with blow-dried hair. "Lesbian chic" looks like the answer to "lesbian invisibility" except that it will only benefit you if you are dating a supermodel. If you are an average lesbian working in a day care center and the local Christian Coalition chapter tries to have you fired and sent to jail, "lesbian chic" will be of no help to you whatsoever.

Lesbian invisibility

Phenomenon of no media attention for the average lesbian who is not chic and probably wears socks with her Tevas.

Politically correct

When you find yourself saying something that you have a sneaking sensation might offend somebody if they took it wrong and you have that "oogly" feeling all over and the conversation stops, you have just said something politically incorrect. Political correctness is a belief system designed to take into consideration the individual experience of everyone on the face of the earth—an ideal that is impossible to fulfill as a human, but, as a lesbian, something to strive for and use to berate others in the community.

"She makes my hood pull back"

"I am attracted to her."

Wankin' widebelt

Slang term for lesbians dating back to post-WWII when certain women refused to give up their hard hats and tool belts to return to the traditional role of homemaker (i.e., "Bill returned from the South Pacific only to find Jean had turned into a wankin' widebelt").

You Might
Be a Lesbian If . . .

ven though at one time or another we have all screamed at our mothers, "This is NOT A PHASE!" the truth is every once in a while we all wonder. A week at the parents', too much Regis and Kathie Lee watching, or a persistent and inexplicable attraction to Jean-Claude Van Damme—any number of things can make even the most hardened lesbian question her sexuality. Luckily for you, the results are finally in from our decade-long study that proves beyond a shadow of a doubt that there are indeed certain signs applicable to basic lesbianism that are UNIVERSAL. This series of highly scientific indicators will help you through those moments of insecurity. Just think of this chapter as a lavender Rorschach test.

You <u>might</u> be a lesbian if...

you are the only girl in your office with
NO FAMILY PICTURES ON YOUR DESK.

You are definitely <u>not</u> a lesbian if...

you think **SAPPHO** was one
of the **MARX BROTHERS.**

You <u>might</u> be a lesbian if . . .

your **HUSBAND** listens to show tunes.

You're definitely <u>not</u> a lesbian if . . .

you would never let your
DOG lick your **FUDGSICLE**.

You <u>might</u> be a lesbian if . . .

your bedside table is equipped
with a **SURGE PROTECTOR**.

You <u>might</u> be a lesbian if . . .

your high school prom dress
was made of **TWEED**.

You <u>might</u> be a lesbian if...

you keep sitting on your college roommate's face "**BY ACCIDENT.**"

You <u>might</u> be a lesbian if...

you have a bumper sticker on your car that says, "I brake for beaver."

You're definitely <u>not</u> a lesbian if...

you think "**BACKLASH**" is a neck injury commonly caused by car accidents.

You're definitely <u>not</u> a lesbian if...

you think "**LABIA MAJORA**" is a country in the former Soviet Union.

You <u>might</u> be a lesbian if...

your hair is short.

your hair is long.

your hair is short on top and long down the back.

your hair is very short all over except for a little braided

tail that emerges from your brain stem.

your nickname is Harry.

your underarms are hairy.

You're definitely <u>not</u> a lesbian if...

you believe a shake is a **MEAL**.

You're definitely <u>not</u> a lesbian if...

you think **MARTINA** is too "mannish."

You <u>might</u> be a lesbian if ...

you think **FAT is a FEMINIST ISSUE**

You <u>might</u> be a lesbian if ...

your first girlfriend's current girlfriend was the
college girlfriend of the woman your
girlfriend just left you for.

You <u>might</u> be a lesbian if ...

you spend a lot of time, effort, and money
TRYING TO GET **PREGNANT**.

You're definitely <u>not</u> a lesbian if ...

you spend a lot of time, effort,
and money **TRYING <u>NOT</u> TO GET PREGNANT.**

PART II

COMING OUT

I-M-L-S-B-N:
A Simple Guide to Accepting Yourself

oming out is to the lesbian what the bar mitz-vah is to the Jew. Like the bar mitzvah, it is a crucial right of passage, marking our entry into the world of the full-grown, emotionally stable homo-sexual female. Unlike the bar mitzvah, when you come out, your family probably won't throw you a big party at the Hilton.

If you're out already, congratulations! If you're still thinking about it, consider the following:

Four Good Reasons to Come Out of the Closet

Reason Number One—
The Money

If you don't believe coming out as a lesbian can be financially profitable, just tell ten people that you are a lesbian and see if they offer you any of the following:

- **A book deal**
- **An appearance on the Jerry Springer Show (which in itself will not get you more money, but you can use it as a platform to help you get more money . . .)**
- **$15,000 from a tabloid to tell them everything you know about Jodie Foster**
- **$25,000 to stay the hell away from their daughter**

Reason Number Two—
Always Felt More Comfortable in the Role of "Pariah"

Being a lesbian automatically excludes you (and your lover) from having to attend boring family events like weddings and holiday dinners. In the event that you are compelled to attend such events, at least you aren't expected to actively socialize with anyone. The one thing that coming out does not exclude you from, oddly enough, is baby-sitting your siblings' children.

Reason Number Three—
Tired of Living at Home

Sometimes it can be hard to tell your parents you're leaving home in a clear, direct manner. Sleeping with your best girlfriend is sort of like sending them a Hallmark card that says, in effect, "Mother, Father, don't you think it's time I got my own apartment?" Whereas most parents would be reluctant to let their fifteen-year-old move to New York City without her high school diploma, nothing will convince them more quickly than finding you in their bed making out with the girl from next door.

Reason Number Four—
Gigantic Clitoris

As an out lesbian, your clitoris might be no bigger than anyone else's, but it will feel bigger (or at least more often).

Nature or Nurture?
More Testimonials from Actual Lesbians

When did you first know you were a lesbian?

💋 "I first knew I was a lesbian when I wanted a GI Joe for Christmas instead of a Barbie. 💋 It was confirmed years later when I wanted two Barbies for some hot, bendable plastic action behind the garage."

Sue P., White Plains, NY

When did you first tell someone?

"Actually, lotsa people told me before I told anyone. In fact, my lesbianism was far advanced—I'd already gotten a girl pregnant—by the time I told my women's studies TA, Gretchen. Gretchen was very understanding, kind of like a lesbian big sister. 💋 She tried to steer me away from the experimenters and the alcoholics, but I had to make my own way."

Rakesha F., Escondido, CA

"I first told Barbie because she knew how to keep her mouth shut 💋 ."

Sue P., White Plains, NY

When did you first act on your lesbian feelings?

"In high school I was terrible at all sports, but ♥ I joined every team I possibly could, from field hockey to badminton. There was always at least one lesbian on every team—with the exception of the drill team—and I managed to be 'best friends' with her for the duration of the season. ♥ We would spend hours driving around in her truck or her Subaru Justy, stocking up on five-pound bags of Three Musketeer bars at the Alpha Beta, which we would devour in a fit of sublimated desire while we pretended to study for chem. ♥ The courtship would culminate in a hot, shame-filled session of mutual masturbation while we watched *Saturday Night Live.* After that, she would shun me virulently, and I would fly solo till track and field started up."

Minne O., Bend, OR

"Technically, my first lesbian experience was of a preschool nature, ♥ when, as a love-struck four-year-old, I would wait for Shelly Brenner to walk past my house each afternoon on her way home from high school so that I might offer her a nice cool glass of milk."

Dawn S., Council Bluffs, IA

Coming-Out Tips for Every Occasion

The saying "It's all in the timing" was first uttered by Plato during one of his lesser-known symposiums to young Greeks on how to come out. Coming out can be awkward and it can happen anywhere at anytime. Here are some helpful *dos* and *don'ts*.

Coming Out Over Meals

Do invite your best friend from high school over and cook her a scrumptious meal.

Don't tell her you are a lesbian while you're brushing crumbs off her blouse.

Coming Out at Weddings

Do bring your girlfriend as your guest.

Don't raise your hand when the minister asks if anyone objects to this union.

Coming Out During the Holidays

Do bring a nice bottle of wine home for the family.

Don't get all drunk and cry about how you'll never get a girlfriend.

Coming Out at Board Meetings

Do firmly protest the homophobic remark the CEO makes by saying, "Sir, I am one of those 'ugly lesbos.'"

Don't stab him in the eye with a sharpened pencil.

When the Eyewitness News Team Features You in Its Pride March Coverage

Do smile proudly for the news cameras.

Don't simulate cunnilingus with your girlfriend for the news cameras.

How do most lesbians come out?
Here are some interesting statistics:

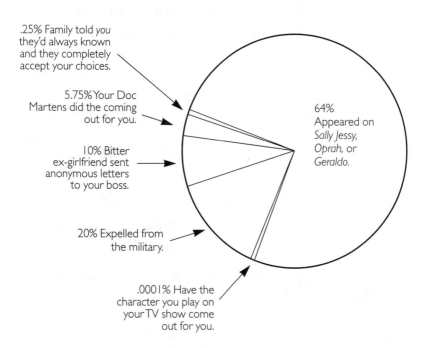

.25% Family told *you* they'd always known and they completely accept your choices.

5.75% Your Doc Martens did the coming out for you.

10% Bitter ex-girlfriend sent anonymous letters to your boss.

64% Appeared on *Sally Jessy, Oprah,* or *Geraldo.*

20% Expelled from the military.

.0001% Have the character you play on your TV show come out for you.

Stupid Family Comments—
Be Prepared

With any luck, in seven or eight years your family will come around and maybe they'll even join PFLAG, but in the meantime, you should be prepared to hear many stupid comments like these actual comments made by actual family members of the Brothers and the Brothers' friends:

"What did I do wrong?"

"Are you the man of the couple?"

"I always knew there was something wrong with you and now I know what it is."

"You just saw what a great life your lesbian sister has and you wanted that too."

"Your father thinks New York City has turned you into a lesbian."

"You're an actress. Why can't you just act straight?"

"I know you already told me that you're gay but I'm using denial and it's working for me."

"What's wrong with the word roommate?"

"Great, next you'll be having sex with animals."

"Well, I'm not surprised. You're half a man anyway."

**"I think
I might
have been
one of them."**

A Game of Luck and Chance

(by **FiveBro, Inc.**)

Number of Players: 2 to 6.
Recommended for: Women only, ages 8 and up.

Pieces required:

2 dice

1 spinner

6 markers: Rainbow flag

           Scottie dog with rainbow flag

           Labrys

           Birkenstock

           Softball mitt

           Honda Accord

50 True Inner Voice cards

50 Society's Rules cards

25 Lucky Break cards

1 Goddess card dispenser (durable plastic)

4 AA batteries (not included)

6 blindfolds

1 bottle of tequila (not included)

1 shot glass (durable plastic)

6 handcuffs (surgical steel)

6 handcuff keys

1 prescription for Thorazine

Set Up

Choose a "Banker."

Put the 4 AA batteries and the Lucky Break cards into the Goddess dispenser.

Fill prescription for Thorazine.

Buy one bottle of tequila (or get someone to buy it for you).

The Object of the Game

The OBJECT OF THE GAME is to GET OUT OF THE CLOSET and STAY OUT OF THE CLOSET, then BEAT THE OTHER PLAYERS TO SAN FRANCISCO OR NEW YORK. The Player that REACHES A BIG CITY WITH $3,500 in her bank (one month's rent plus a security deposit) WINS THE GAME!

How to Play

1. Players START IN THE CLOSET. Each Player gets a STARTING BANK OF $400.
2. A Player must ROLL A DOUBLE SIX to GET OUT OF THE CLOSET.
3. Once a Player is OUT, she must BUY A TICKET that will direct her to NEW YORK or SAN FRANCISCO. (TICKETS COST $400 and are NONREFUNDABLE.)
4. Player then proceeds toward her destination ONE SQUARE AT A TIME!
5. Get ready for some big laughs as the luck of the draw helps determine which player will WIN THE GAME!

Rules

What to Do if You Land on a Pink Triangle: Player must draw a card from the True Inner Voice deck and follow the instructions on the card!

Sample Inner Voice Cards:

You have a lesbian aunt, take a Lucky Break card!

You hold hands with your girlfriend in the Kmart, move ahead three spaces!

You steal a woman from her husband, send another Player back into the CLOSET!

You successfully argue a gay rights case before the Supreme Court. FLY DIRECTLY TO SAN FRANCISCO!

You take a women's studies course, GO AGAIN!

You get fired from the Cracker Barrel, take $10,000 in punitive damages!

What to Do If You Land on an American Flag: Player must draw a card from the Society's Rules deck and follow the instructions on the card!

Sample Society's Rules Cards:

You have Fundamentalist parents. SKIP A TURN!

You tell your aunt you're "almost engaged." START OVER!

You wear a "Pussy Power" T-shirt to your high school reunion, but turn it inside out when you get there. MOVE BACK THREE SPACES!

Your mother reads your diary. Go to the MENTAL INSTITUTION!

When a Player Lands in the Bar: When a Player stumbles into the lesbo BAR she must SPIN THE SPINNER to determine how many SHOTS OF TEQUILA she must drink before she can move ahead.[1] She must remain in the BAR until she spins TWELVE-STEP.

---

1. WARNING! Some studies indicate that alcohol may be hazardous to your health if not used properly. FiveBro, Inc., cannot be held liable for any injury, accident, side effects, hangover, or brain damage that may occur as a result of playing Coming Out on Top.

When a Player Lands in Jail: When a Player lands in JAIL, she must SPIN THE SPINNER, while wearing the handcuffs, to determine how many times she must SERVICE THE MATRON before she is released.

When a Player Lands in the Mental Institution: When a Player lands in the MENTAL INSTITUTION, she must SPIN THE SPINNER to determine her DOSAGE. Player must then TAKE HER THORAZINE[2] or if she spins THERAPY, she can PAY $90 and MOVE ON. Players who have landed in the MENTAL INSTITUTION must PAY $90 ON EVERY SUBSEQUENT TURN. (NOTE: If a Player cannot PAY THE $90, Player must go back to the MENTAL INSTITUTION and SPIN AGAIN!)

When a Player Lands in a Heterosexual Marriage: Player must SPIN THE SPINNER to determine how many years of HETEROSEXUAL DRUDGERY she must endure. Player must then WEAR A BLINDFOLD until her MARRIAGE IS OVER. If a Player spins a DIVORCE, she can move ahead two spaces and COLLECT $10,000 IN ALIMONY.

Lucky Break:

When a Player lands on a PINK TRIANGLE that says LUCKY BREAK, she must SNATCH a card from the Goddess dispenser. A Player can play her LUCKY BREAK card right away or HOLD ON

---

2. WARNING! Thorazine is a powerful drug and should not be taken without a prescription (prescription included). DO NOT TAKE WITH ALCOHOL. FiveBro, Inc., cannot be held liable for any injury, accident, side effects, lasting side effects, or brain damage, or other permanent injury that may occur as a result of playing Coming Out on Top.

TO IT for later! (NOTE: If a Player draws a Joker from the Lucky Break deck, Player must GO DIRECTLY TO JAIL!)

Sample Lucky Break Cards

Find a good therapist, MOVE AHEAD THREE SPACES.

Parents accept you, TAKE $200.

Parents die, TAKE $100,000.

You find a job where you get to wear pants to work. SPIN AGAIN.

GOOD LUCK!!!

Once Upon a Lesbian

 oming out is usually either a fairy tale or a horror story. You might be magically transported to the Land of Love and Acceptance, as in these classic tales:

"Snow White and the Seven Dykes":

These women whistled even while they weren't working and it wasn't long before Snow White caught on.

"Puss 'n' Motorcycle Boots":

This woman loved her Harley so much she couldn't think of anything else . . . until she met the handsome lady mechanic of her dreams.

"Thumbelina":

Little Thumbelina's world breaks wide open when she meets her cousin, Fistalina.

Or your story might be a SCARY one, like these:

"The Mother Who Cried Herself to Death":

Mother dies of dehydration two weeks after daughter brings her girlfriend home for Thanksgiving dinner.

"The Brother (Who Thought You Were) from Another Planet":

The story of the brother who thinks it's cool that you're a "lesbo freak" and he constantly wants to show you off to all his friends.

"The Telltale Heart":

The true story of a married woman whose heart pounded furiously every time she hugged a woman.

"And Then There Were None":

Shirley told one friend she was a lesbian and soon no one was returning her phone calls.

If All Else Fails . . .

f all else fails, you can always go back into the closet. Your mother never believed you were really a lesbian anyway.

PART III

RELATIONSHIPS (FINDING HER AND KEEPING HER)

Where the Girls Are
(How to Sight That Perfect Girl in Your Curly Crosshairs)

Okay. You're ready to begin your new, exciting life as a lesbian. There's just one thing you're missing—a babe. Here's a list of some of the most likely spots to find that special someone:

COMMUNITY CENTERS: Community centers are ideal for you, novice lesbian, because your "gaydar" is probably not well-honed yet. You need to be in a setting where you can be 99 percent certain that the woman you are about to proposition is a lesbian. Otherwise, that cute woman in the subway with the short haircut might slap you in the face when you ask her out. At the center, you run the risk of hitting on some cute little fags at first, but they are usually nice about it.

LIBRARIES: Libraries are a lesbian's happy hunting ground. Stake out a desk near the women's lit. section or the gay/lesbian section and you will be like a bear in a beehive. A request for access to the Rare Book Room will also get you access to the foxy head librarian.

BARS: It used to be that 95 percent of all lesbians met in bars. With the increased popularity of twelve-step groups, that number has decreased significantly (except in some rural areas). Look for bars with names like Shadows, Backstreets, and The Purple Iris (see "Closety Bar Names" in Part VIII). Drink little and tip big and you can get the bartender to help you sort the "maybes" from the "you bets."

MUSIC FESTIVALS: Music festivals are a great initiation for the brand-new lesbian. The most compelling feature of these events, besides the fact they are generally women only, is that there is a great deal of nakedness, giving you ample time to lean up against a tree and speculate on how much fun the rest of your life is going to be. A downside is that after three or four days of living on beans and tofu, your tent is uninhabitable.

SPORTS LEAGUES: Sports are a great way to look for personality traits in people. You're attracted to that cute center on your basketball team and you're thinking about asking her on a date—but wait. Watch how she reacts in the fourth quarter with three seconds on the clock and it's all down to her. If she turns into a monster, take a second look at that forward or that guard. A well-adjusted personality can be very attractive.

GROUP THERAPY: Under no circumstances should you date another woman in your therapy group. Look elsewhere, lesbian!

TWELVE-STEP GROUPS: Twelve-step groups are not like group therapy. You can date someone in your twelve-step program provided—and this is important—that you are within three or four steps of each other. In other words, advanced twelve-steppers and novices do not mix. You will get into that caretaker/helpless child routine, driving you deeper into the destructive behavior you were doing so well at overcoming in the first place.

EXERCISE YARD: You're new to prison and everybody's probably paired up already. Don't fear. Use your time in the exercise yard to impress the local gals with your physical prowess. Soon some little honey will abandon her tired old girlfriend for your fresh blood. Just be prepared to fight for love and don't let anyone know you're doing time for stealing a stapler from the office supply closet.

MESS TENT: You might not have known you were a lesbian when you joined the army. You just thought you liked to wear a uniform and work with your hands. But now that you're here, it's all starting to make sense. Now your only problem is how to tell the butches from the femmes when everyone is dressed the same.

CONVENT: You might not have known you were a lesbian when you joined the convent. You thought you were really in love with Jesus Christ. But now you find that when fingering your beads, your mind seems to wander to Sister Mary Stuart's nipples. Take our word for it. You're not thinking about anything Mother Superior hasn't thought about already. Convents have been hotbeds of lesbian activity throughout the ages (where many a lesbian's prayer has been answered). What makes it so exciting is that it is oh-so-forbidden, and because both of you believe in God, you'll always feel as if someone is watching.

PERSONAL ADS: Personal ads are not the pathetic mark of the loser that they used to be. They really work! You just have to know how to read between the lines. For example:

"Bi-curious" really means "Husband wants a three-way."

"Likes sports" equals "Likes to eat Doritos while watching the Super Bowl."

"Discreet" and "Straight acting" reads "Closeted."

"For possible life partner" is "Looking for someone to pay the mortgage."

"Cuddle and take long walks on the beach" translates "Wants sex."

"Seeks butch top for hot, wild spanking session" is really "Likes to cuddle and take long walks on the beach."

INTRODUCTION THROUGH FRIENDS: Though this technique can be successful, we urge you to consider the following scenario: Your friends, Pat and Linda, are so excited to set you up on a date with their friend Michelle. Sounds terrific! But before you launch yourself into this loaded situation, ask yourself these questions: (1) Do you think that Pat and Linda have a good relationship? (2) Are you the only decent friend Pat and Linda have? (3) Is this the same Michelle that Pat broke up with two years ago because she could only have sex while talking to her mom on the phone?

ABSTINENCE: The best pickup line in all of history is to tell a woman, "I've given up on sex." She will respond immediately because deep in her heart every lesbian knows that she can fix virtually anything. The tragic downside of the abstinence technique is that you have to really mean it. Once you give in, the magic is gone.

CRUISES: What better way to score a chick than to book yourself passage on an ocean liner full of dykes. The sun. The salt air. The happy hour. All virtually guarantee you will find someone desperate enough to at least cuddle you.

INTEREST/ACTIVITY GROUPS: If you live in a large metropolitan area, you can probably find an interest group with a name like Brunch Bunnies or Wilderness Wymyn. These groups afford you a good opportunity to really get to know someone while engaging in a fun activity. For instance, if you are in a wilderness group, you can check out the butt of the girl hiking in front of you.

INTERNET: Many a happy couple have met in cyberspace. We suggest a face-to-face meeting ASAP to ensure that your new girlfriend is not, in fact, your new creepy voyeur boyfriend.

Recognizing Lesbians in a "Hostile Environment"

Think you're ready to move up to some more "advanced" cruising? Here are some tips on skimmin' for wimmin in "straight" settings.

1. **At the office:** You're in the office, where all women are forced into rigid dress codes. It can be difficult to distinguish the rug-munchers from the rest. A woman walks by. Is her gait a little broad? Does she look as if she thinks her pantyhose are really sweat pants? Is that cute little headband sitting atop a crew cut? If she asks you to accompany her to the rest room while she freshens her ChapStick, our advice is . . . GO!

2. **At a wedding:** You're at that bastion of heterosexism, the Wedding. All the women are wearing lime green. How will you ever possibly tell? At the reception, pay close attention: Who's eating cake with her very own bowie knife?

3. **Shopping:** You've stopped at a Wal-Mart in the nation's heartland to replenish your supply of propane canisters. You spot a sensible-looking gal in aisle three perusing the fishing tackle. Her hair is cropped close, she's sporting a comfy flannel shirt, and her work boots are sturdy. Looks like family, you say. Not so fast! You're in Iowa, where women of all persuasions look deceivingly homosexual. We suggest you give her the Brothers' "Midwest Test": saunter up to her with your shopping cart and politely ask where the canned tuna is located. If she sniffs her fingers, you know you're in luck!

In the Beginning
(How to Handle a Woman)

S o you've met a girl and you've started dating. Congratulations! But beware of these most common pitfalls:

Don't say "I love you" the first time you have sex. You will be tempted, but DON'T DO IT! A lesbian will seize onto the words "I love you" like a pit bull and hold you to it forever or until she meets another woman who makes the same mistake, whichever happens first. If you find yourself swept away in the moment, try these alternatives:

a. I love . . . this bed.

b. I love . . . that smell.

c. I love . . . your hairdo.

Don't talk about your cats. Calm down. This doesn't mean never. But it's important that your prospective new girlfriend doesn't think that you don't have any human friends. Limit yourself to mentioning the cats once or twice per encounter, at least until the girlfriend has had a chance to bond with them as well.

Don't go into couples' counseling (yet). If after the first few dates you are discussing couples' counseling, you can be relatively sure this relationship is not the best thing for you or for her at this time. In other words, you have made a big, BIG mistake and you need to get out now.

What's a Little Sex Between Friends?

You and Melanie have been friends for almost two years. She's cute and smart, and her experimental videos are really interesting. "Maybe Melanie'd make a good girlfriend," you find yourself thinking. The Five Lesbian Brothers advise you to sit down and have a good long think over this.

Questions to ask yourself:

1. When was the last time I had sex?

2. Is my eyeglass prescription still good?

3. Was I sober when the idea first occurred to me?

Not that many happy couples weren't formed from the "She was right there in my own backyard the whole time!" phenomenon. It does happen. But as Sappho once said, "A hand in the bush is nice, but not worth losing a friend over." Why are we so hell-bent on having sex with every girl in our circle, anyway? Unless you live in a very small town, there is no excuse for this behavior. A friendship untainted by the exchange of body fluids can be very refreshing.

Five Surefire Signs of Sexual Attraction

1. Your hood pulls back (see glossary).

2. Your underwear sticks to the ceiling.

3. That embarrassing wet spot on the upholstery.

4. Your nipples poke through your down vest.

5. You spontaneously eject your tampon.

Seven Typical Lesbian Dates

1. Dinner ⇒ movie ⇒ sex ⇒ move in together.

2. Softball game ⇒ shower ⇒ ex ⇒ move in together.

3. County fair ⇒ hayride ⇒ sex ⇒ move in together.

4. Estimate ⇒ oil change ⇒ lube job ⇒ sex ⇒ move in together.

5. Reveille ⇒ fifteen-mile hike ⇒ sex ⇒ obstacle course ⇒ sex in a bunker ⇒ dishonorable discharge.

6. Pray ⇒ pray ⇒ feed the poor ⇒ sex ⇒ go to confession.

7. Breakfast ⇒ shower ⇒ cavity check ⇒ sex ⇒ back to your cell.

The Brothers' Mailbox

You thought when you found the perfect girl it would all be smooth sailing. Unfortunately, relationships are never easy and we lesbians don't get instruction manuals with ours the way the straight people do. That's why the Five Lesbian Brothers spend hours every day answering the pleas for advice sent to us by lesbians from around the country. Here are some typical questions sent in by typical lesbian couples.

Dear Five Lesbian Brothers:

My lover and I have been together for... well, that's exactly the problem. She says we've been together for a year this coming Sunday and I say we've been together for four months. The thing is, we slept together once a year ago when she was breaking up with her ex-girlfriend. Then she got back together with her for two months and then she needed another month on her own to get back in touch with her autonomy. Then we dated for three weeks with no sex or even kissing (her idea!) and then we finally slept together and four months ago we moved in together. The problem is, when is our anniversary? She says it's the first time we slept together. I say it's when we actually moved in with each other. This is causing a lot of controversy. Please help.

Lost in Louisville

Dear Lost:

Get out from under the "If I'm right, she's wrong" mentality and let your true commitment shine. Relationships are about compromise. We say there aren't near-enough celebratory dates in our community and suggest that you celebrate any and all of the milestones in your relationship. Remember, you don't have to be ruled by the oppressive patriarchal norms of the dominant culture. Whatever you want to celebrate can be celebrated—the first time she looked at you in that special way, the first time you scratched her back, the first time she left the bathroom door open.... You get the idea. Celebrate!!!

Dear Five Lesbian Brothers:

Recently my lover and I attended a cocktail party at my law firm. The next week we attended her cousin's wedding. These two events may seem completely unrelated but we had the same problem in both situations. Neither one of us knew how to introduce the other to co-workers, clients, or distant relatives. I thought of using the word <u>partner</u> but then I worried that my boss would hear a rumor that I was leaving to start my own practice. The word <u>lover</u> seemed too personal for a work situation. Conversely, at the wedding, the phrase <u>significant</u> <u>other</u> just would not cut it. These two events left us feeling hopeless about ever finding the right word to describe our relationship to other people. What do you suggest?

Puzzled in Provincetown

Dear Puzz:

This is one of the biggest problems for lesbians worldwide. As you point out there are a number of possibilities ranging from "significant other" to "120 pounds on the end of my arm," but there's no all-occasion moniker. That's why we suggest when introducing your lady love you rattle off all the possible terms until you see that look that says, "I think I know what you're trying to tell me but I'm not too comfortable with it so I'm going to try to totally freeze all the muscles in my face." Then you'll know you've made yourself clear.

Dear Five Lesbian Brothers:

My lover and I have been together for seven years. We moved in together after one year and by the end of that year we had stopped having sex. This is really starting to get on my nerves. Are other couples like this? I am afraid to ask my friends because I don't want them to think that I never have sex (which I don't). Please help me.

Celibate in Cincinnati

Dear Celibate:

Isn't it funny how all of the people who write to us have alliterative names? This is just something for you to ponder in order to get your mind off your terrible problem of lesbian bed death. Lesbian bed death is real. It does exist. And you and your girlfriend have it. But it doesn't have to be terminal. Remember, Lazarus rose from the dead and he was only a man. You and your lover are going to have to take some serious steps to resuscitate this part of your relationship. Start by talking about why it took you five years to start getting irritated. Second, try taking large doses of testosterone.

Dear Five Lesbian Brothers:

My girlfriend, Rosita, always wants to go to her parents' house for the holidays but I am a goddess-worshiping pagan. I love my girlfriend and I know it's important for her to see her family, but I can't take the patriarchal religious rituals they lay on me, plus I'm a vegan and they always serve big animal flesh hunks. What can I do?

Bah Humbug in Brooklyn

Dear Bah:

Does your girlfriend accompany you on your holidays? We're willing to bet she cheerfully attends any number of naked drumming rituals and makes all the millet-tofu bars for your coven's solstice party. So be nice to her parents and try to just fill up on mashed potatoes.

Dear Five Lesbian Brothers:

I hardly know where to begin. It is all so awful. They are probably right. My girlfriend, Denise, never had a serious lesbian relationship before me. Now her parents blame ME for turning her queer! They say their little girl could be married to Dr. Wayne Marquart by now and that they could have a grandson on the way and all the free dental work they could use and that I stole that from them and made them ashamed and put twenty years on their lives and that poor Wayne is living in a trailer park, a broken man. Are they right? I'm a bad seed and I've grown up all over Cindy like a vine and squished every chance for true happiness out of her.

Blown Away in Burlington

Dear Blown:

You know who we would like to blow away, don't you? Denise's parents! They've really done a number on you. Listen to us, because we know. You're probably way down at the bottom of a long list of people targeted for blame by Denise's parents. We say smile and accept the credit.

Dear Five Lesbian Brothers:

My mom says I don't have a dad but my biology teacher Mr. Moss says that is impossible. My other mom, I call her Ruth, says Mom just can't remember who Dad is, and when Mom heard that she and Ruth got into a terrible fight. What's the big deal? Can you explain it all to me?

Daddyless in Dry Gulch

Dear Kid:

Don't feel guilty. Okay, you can feel guilty if you must because we don't want to tell you not to have your feelings but what we can tell you is that Mr. Moss is part right. Not everyone has a father, but everyone DOES have a sperm donor. And if you really want to see a terrible fight, see what happens on the school board when Mr. Moss starts teaching THAT in school!

PART IV

FILLING UP AND SPILLING OVER (SEX AND THE LESBIAN)

What Lesbians Do in Bed
Three Objective Scientific Studies

Penthouse Magazine
Survey, June 1993 Issue:

79% Have sex with straight couples

10% "69" with a man watching

10% "69" with a man participating

1% Sex with animals

Woman's Day
Survey, July 1994 Issue:

96% Not sure

2% Hug?

2% Kiss?

Entertainment Weekly
Survey, November 1993 Issue:

68% Kill men with ice picks

20% Commit suicide

6% Whisper in French

6% Caress unidentifiable body parts while whispering in French

List of Common
Sex Injuries/Hazards

1. Broken wrist

2. Broken jaw

3. Choking

4. Hair balls

5. Tongue cramp

6. Rug burns

7. Lockjaw

8. Deviated septum

9. Torn earlobe

Monogamy vs. Nonmonogamy
A Volatile Point/Counterpoint

onogamy is for sex-negative squares. The Five Lesbian Brothers fit snugly into that category and we won't deny it. So to help round out this round table discussion, we've invited our local S/M, prosex youngster, who bluntly calls herself Cock, to offer the argument for nonmonogamy.

Five Lesbian Brothers: So, Cock, isn't it kind of dangerous? Having sex with all different kinds of people?

Cock: Hey, life is dangerous. I could get hit by a cable car tomorrow. Besides, I practice safe sex religiously.

Five Lesbian Brothers: Besides STDs, what about when your girlfriend gets mad?

Cock: Hey, I don't cheat on my sex partners. Everyone knows the deal before we play.

Five Lesbian Brothers: What about intimacy and all that emotional fulfillment and stuff?

Cock: My friends and I would do anything for each other. There's no intimacy greater than letting someone cut you with a razor. What about you? Are you emotionally fulfilled?

Five Lesbian Brothers: Well, see, being with the same person, night after night, day after day, and knowing that that's the way it's going to be forever, you develop a real . . . uh . . . a kind of . . . closeness, I guess you'd say.

Cock: Blazing resentment is more like it. I'd rather be free to express my love in whatever form it takes.

Five Lesbian Brothers: Well, it's not resentment, really. It's more like a test. A sacrifice that brings you closer. It's like the Indigo Girls say, "The closer I'm bound in love to you, the closer I am to free."

Cock: Bondage. Hm. I can relate to that.

Five Lesbian Brothers: Cock, I guess the thing is we're scared. What if we get up in that sling and we don't feel aroused, only a little chilly?

Cock: Projecting boredom is a sign of a repressed desire to be caned. I know, because I used to be like that.

Five Lesbian Brothers: You? Cock, that's hard to believe. You look like you were born with that ball in your tongue.

Cock: Hell, no. I, too, was laden with the baggage of antisex hegemony. I didn't give my first spanking till I was nineteen.

Five Lesbian Brothers: Well, that makes us feel a lot better. Thanks.

Lesbian Sex—
It Isn't Just with Women Anymore!

Back in the seventies, the standards for being a lesbian were a lot tougher. If you slept with a man, you were OUT OF THE CLUB. Young lesbians today don't know how easy they've got it. They sleep with whoever they want and then sit right in the front row at an Alix Dobkin concert. Not wanting to stand in the way of progress, the Brothers have compiled some pros and cons of mating outside the species. Here's what you should consider if you're thinking of sleeping with . . .

A LESBIAN
> Pro: She probably won't gag when she goes down on you.
> Con: She might not take her softball mitt off.

A BISEXUAL
> Pro: She'll insist on safer sex.
> Con: She'll insist on safer sex.

A MARRIED COUPLE
> Pro: They might buy you dinner.
> Con: Could be fatal when the wife likes you better and the husband tries to run you over with his Pathfinder.

A STRAIGHT WOMAN
> Pro: Hot in bed.
> Con: Cold in public.

A STRAIGHT MAN

>Pro: Will watch the football game with you afterward.
>
>Con: This dildo has a shelf-life.

A GAY MAN

>Pro: Will help you work through your anal shame.
>
>Con: Gerbil.

A CO-WORKER

>Pro: Sex during lunch.
>
>Con: No lunch!

A STRANGER

>Pro: The thrill of anonymity.
>
>Con: Your bunny might get boiled.

A GROUP

>Pro: All those holes!
>
>Con: Losing your keys in the clothes pile.

FOR MONEY

>Pro: You get money!
>
>Con: Your pimp gets 90 percent.

YOURSELF

>Pro: No strings attached.
>
>Con: Hairy palms.

Sex Toys in a Pinch!
The Five Lesbian Brothers
Recommend:

Carrots

Cucumbers

Tickle deodorant

Shower massage

Bicycle seat

Pony

Electric toothbrush

Anything with a motor, really. If you're desperate enough,
you can lean up against the clothes dryer.

PART V

BREAKING UP
IS HARD TO DO

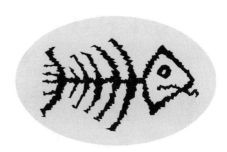

The Seven Deadly Signs
(How to Tell It's Over)

1. Your girlfriend tells you she's always assumed your relationship was nonmonogamous.

2. You find Post-it notes in the refrigerator that say things like "my carob soy milk."

3. You realize you know her back like the palm of your hand.

4. You realize you know the palm of your hand really, really well.

5. Your couples' counselor is seen dancing with your girlfriend at Whispers.

6. Your cat starts to take sides.

7. Your girlfriend's sister calls, and when you answer, she says, "Oh, are you still there?"

The "Ex"-Files

Lesbians use the term *ex-girlfriend,* but those in the know realize that it means very little. While in some special cases the moniker actually sticks for good, most lesbian breakups only last somewhere between a few moments in a heated argument to a few years. The following are some case histories illustrating this particular pathology. The examples are purely random and are in no way reflective of the personal experiences of the Five Lesbian Brothers.

Case # 1: Xavia (not her real name),

thirty-two, living in Freeport, Long Island.

Xavia was in a relationship for three months with Hilda, a beer and softball lesbian. They had dated during the softball season, but when Hilda's team got into the championship series, Hilda sobered up a bit and decided that Xavia was not for her. Xavia, distraught, decided to ignore Hilda's declaration of separation. She continued to call Hilda and show up at the games and act like they were still together. Eventually, Hilda forgot that she had even broken up with Xavia.

𝕮𝖆𝖘𝖊 #2: 𝖃𝖊𝖓𝖎𝖆 (𝖓𝖔𝖙 𝖍𝖊𝖗 𝖗𝖊𝖆𝖑 𝖓𝖆𝖒𝖊, 𝖇𝖚𝖙 𝖕𝖗𝖊𝖙𝖙𝖞 𝖈𝖑𝖔𝖘𝖊),

twenty-seven, living in San Francisco.

Xenia moved to California from a small town in Maine after a nasty breakup with her first girlfriend, Clara, involving an illicit affair with one of the couple's "best friends." Xenia hoped the move would help her forget about Clara and get on with her life. Imagine her surprise, as Holly Near so eloquently said, when soon after unpacking her boxes, she ran into Clara on the corner of Eighteenth and Mission. Xenia, frozen in shock at the sight of Clara, did hardly protest when Clara approached her and whispered fiercely into her ear, "I'm ready to commit now, I want you," and carried her off to a movie theater where they had public sex.

𝕮𝖆𝖘𝖊 #3: 𝖃𝖊𝖓𝖔𝖇𝖎𝖆 (𝖍𝖊𝖗 𝖗𝖊𝖆𝖑 𝖓𝖆𝖒𝖊),

forty-eight, living in Atlanta.

Xenobia had just ended the twenty-sixth relationship of her life and was as devastated as she had been with the other twenty-five. Once again, she had been summarily rejected as "too clingy" after chasing girlfriend number twenty-six's car through the streets of Atlanta by bus and on foot for more than two hours. Looking at herself in the mirror, mascara running and false eyelashes partially unglued, she said to herself, "I'm an old hag and I'll never do this again." In this particular case, Xenobia was actually able to keep to her word as she returned to men and got hooked up with an organization full of guys who dig former lesbians.

Case #4: Xandra (her real name if it started with an X),

thirty-four, living in San Bernardino.

Xandra, a well-meaning but thoroughly checked-out lesbian management trainee, had been in San Bernardino for more than a year and had not gone out on a single date. She knew hardly any other lesbians and had no idea what they looked like in Southern California. When she received a note from Harriet, an "ex" of hers back in Tallahassee, she got on a plane and soon the two were rejoined. Xandra found that she liked the familiarity of Harriet, but didn't like the "hassle" of having to "relate" to someone else. So she broke up with Harriet and she got back together with her first girlfriend, Cybil. Cybil didn't seem quite right either, so she moved on to Sarah, yet another of her past loves. Predictably, this "ex" became an "ex" yet again as Xandra plowed up the entire field of her past in a pathetic terminal cycle of searching where she had already looked before.

Coping Skills

O kay. She dumped you. You thought it was going to last forever but it didn't. So you dust yourself off, square your shoulders, and move on. Life is a journey. We have only today. You're being prepared for something better.

But *first* you must wallow in the mire of self-pity for a few years. Some favorite lesbian coping skills are:

- Obsessive nostalgia for past relationships, which can turn to Stalking (see below).
- Excessive eating, drinking, and/or drugging.
- New girlfriend as soon as possible.
- Random and superficial sex encounters.

The Five Lesbian Brothers do not recommend any one of these strategies—they all work equally well. Choose the one that most appeals to you.

The Lesbian Stalker

A ccording to FBI statistics, one in five lesbian relationships that end "nonmutually" result in the dangerous phenomenon known as stalking. This situation occurs when the jilted party is "unhappy" and wishes reconciliation. Statistics show that this obsession with getting back together is often a delusional fantasy. Take the case of Lucy, a Stalker from Idaho, who followed her ex-lover around for six years, undaunted by an order of protection, two Dobermans, and an electric fence. Finally, her former lover moved all the way to Alaska. The Stalker interpreted the move as a sign of true love since they had once flown over the state together in a plane.

Here are the warning signs that one of your ex-lovers is turning into a Stalker:

- Repeated unexplained hang-ups on the phone.

- Answering machine message tape entirely taken up by one long recording of your favorite Joan Jett album left by "anonymous" caller.

- "Coincidental" meetings with Stalker in places like your driveway or backyard.

- Tearful late-night phone requests to "come over and cut me down off the rafters."

- Mysterious deliveries of cases of your cat's favorite food.

- Returning home from work to find "her" chores done, even though you took away her keys.

- Finding your ex and her "new girlfriend" drunk and making out in your car.

- Obsessive rants from Stalker about how the president is keeping Jodie Foster from returning her phone calls.

The Divorce Settlement

e can't legally get married, but we do it anyway. So when we break up, we might as well formally divorce. Here is a sample document to help you through this painful time.

Let it heretofore be known that as of _____ __, 199_, _____ (name of 1st party) and _____ (name of 2nd party) are dissolving their Union, never recognized by the State but at one time by the Goddess. The Party in the First Part, being the Rascal who was having an affair with her Soccer Coach for six months, does hereby forgo all rights and claims to the: (1) big screen TV, (2) carpeted cat tree, (3) autographed Meg Christian CD, and (4) favorite bridge partners. The Party in the Second Part, being the Long-Suffering Co-dependent, does hereby retain all rights and assigns to Deborah, their Couples' Counselor, and Diversions, their local dive.

In the question of Isis, their tabby, and Gaia, the Labrador, custody is awarded to the Party in the Second Part, in accordance with the Penal Code, Section 36, Paragraph 1, which states that in the absence of any evidence to the contrary, custody of Animal Companions shall rest with the primary care giver. The Party in the First Part shall retain unsupervised weekend visiting rights, and is hereby obligated to provide said Animal Companions with numerous Chew Toys and Catnip Mice, the frequency of which shall not be less than thrice yearly.

PART VI

"LESBOPOLITAN"
(A GUIDE TO
LESBIAN STYLE)

A Room of One's Own

How many lesbians have you seen featured in the pages of *House and Garden?* None, you say? That's probably because when it comes to home decor, gay men were endowed with all the talent. Though we lesbians may not have the most stylish subculture in the world, that doesn't mean we don't try. If you're thinking of redecorating and you want your home to reflect a special "lesbian flair," consider one or more of these options:

1. The Little Boy's Room

   Elements: Bunk beds, model airplanes, football helmet swag lamp.

   Pros: Neat stuff.

   Cons: She's on top, you're on the bottom, but you don't sleep together.

2. Parents' Basement

   Elements: Wood paneling, sofa bed, cardboard closet, Oriental screen to hide the furnace.

   Pros: You have your own entrance.

   Cons: Everyone has to walk through your room to get to the laundry.

3. The Communal House

Elements: Tofu cheese press, sprouts growing in bathroom cabinet, batik wall hangings, macramé fire escape ladder.

Pros: All the housework is equally divided.

Cons: You end up doing all the work.

4. The Fixer-Upper

Elements: Heavy-duty plastic on windows, dishes washed in bathroom, exposed asbestos.

Pros: You get to have everything just the way you want it.

Cons: You have to *make* everything just the way you want it.

5. The Tepee

Elements: Fire pit, bed of fresh straw.

Pros: You're very close to nature.

Cons: Nature is very close to you.

6. Bachelorette

Elements: Big giant bed, tiny kitchen, refrigerator contains Diet Pepsi and two-year-old can of macadamia nuts.

Pros: You can bring a babe home anytime.

Cons: First she has to agree.

7. The Happy Couple

Elements: Two dog beds, cat door, framed domestic partnership certificate, couch with two deep indents from your recently developed "lesbian big butts."

Pros: Comfy.

Cons: Smells like cat pee.

8. Just Like Mom and Dad

Identical to "The Happy Couple" but with cocktails.

Shockingly Expensive

Items for sale from the Brothers' catalogue

Martina lawn ornaments

So you've decided to leave the gay ghetto and move to suburbia. Could anything make you feel more proud as a lesbian homeowner than this set of adorable Martina lawn ornaments?

wrought-iron bench

You've always wanted to sit on Martina. Now's your chance! *Handcrafted by lesbian-friendly artisans in New Mexico.* **$8,098.**

bird bath and fountain

As this miniature Martina draws back a well-developed arm to return the serve of her hapless opponent, fine droplets of sweat rain down from her underarm and beneath her sweatband into a replica of the trophy at Wimbledon. A delight for bird and babe watchers alike! Bronze. *Hand-forged in Palo Alto, CA, by Rena.* **$12,045.**

Martina bug zapper.

Yeeow! You know she was good at slaughtering her opponents! Wait until you see what she can do with the mosquitoes in your backyard! Be out, proud, AND bug free! *Specially made for Shockingly Expensive! by Carlucci's Pest Control of Queens.* **$647.**

come to MY window (bird feeder)

Birds will be attracted to your window by this finely wrought wire sculpture of lesbian superstar Melissa Etheridge, who will have robins and sparrows alike eating out of the palms of her hands. Real human hair cascades down this wire Melissa's back. It's an ecologically sound nesting material and all that blond hair is as irresistible to birds as it is to Melissa fans. If you're a lesbian who enjoys nature (and what lesbian doesn't?), you must have Melissa in your window. **$400.**

Dan White's twinkie mix

If you can't beat homophobia, why not have a laugh at it? These delicious little cakes are guaranteed to "drive you nuts." A great gift to lighten the mood of anyone feeling particularly oppressed.

twinkies: $8 ea. or $27 for package of 3.

one of our most popular items is back

Sweep away shame with these rainbow gay pride vacuum cleaner bags! **3 for $27.**

for the office . . .
"scream" saver

Finally ready to come out at work? Have you had it with insensitive co-workers asking you when you're going to get a boyfriend? Celebrate national coming-out day this year in style with this hysterical and proud screen saver. **"I like PUSSY, damn it! Mind your own damn business from now on!" $121.**

placenta paperweight

Honor the birth of your artificially inseminated child with your or your partner's placenta frozen forever in amber glass. **$865.**

lesbian buns calendar

You've heard of lesbian chic. Well, this is lesbian "cheek"! 12 months of beautiful lesbian backsides of all shapes and colors! What better way to get your lifestyle included in the chitchat around the water cooler. **$39.**

new item!

Let's face it. The whole country, gay and straight, is moving to the right. That's why we're offering this new line of items which features that adorable dinosaur Barney and the 100% nonconfrontational plea, "Please don't hate us because we're gay." Even Anita Bryant can't resist Barney, right? For the apologist in all of us.

fine calfskin briefcase—$432.

sterling silver tie tack—$112.

cellular phone—$385.

just for you . . .
hot/cold vaginal pride mug

Put your lips to our lips by enjoying your favorite beverage from this mug specially designed with the vagina in mind. **$41.**

Russian roulette insemination tampons

These 100% biodegradable tampons put the "surprise" back in pregnancy. If you're one of those women who want to get pregnant but feel you're not financially equipped or emotionally ready, if you envy straight women who can get pregnant "by accident," then these tampons with a specially designed "spermy tip" on every seventh tampon are for you. Box of 48 tampons and dry ice packaging, **$564.**

literary selections
hunk love

by Swen and Tom Hunter-Lundstein.

The inspiring story of these two well-known body building e.s.l. instructors—their love and their lives together as well as their successful chinchilla farm in which the animals are taught to use computers and donated to arthritis sufferers worldwide. *Hardcover. 85 full-color photos.* **$75.**

sweating and eating fried foods

by Dolores Abigail.

This acclaimed lesbian writer tells the story of "Toe," a working-class girl growing up in the Deep South. *Pocket edition.* **$9.75**

lower east side, lesbians and stuff

by Susan Schulberg.

". . . I lay facedown on the tar beach with a pastrami sandwich from Katz's thinking about last night's protest march and how I'd like to smash my ex-girlfriend's hands in a car door. She deserves it." *Cloth-bound.* **$30.**

the unabridged Sappho

Mary Howard-Smith, ed.

Greek scholars working day and night have restored many of the previously "lost" fragments of the work of the great poet. For example, the fragment:

"I ask you, sir, to
stand face to face
with me as a friend

would: show me the
favor of your eyes"

now bears the recently translated ending:

"or I'll cut your dick off." *Paper.* **$12.95**

Queersine:
What Lesbians Eat:
The Great Junk Food vs. Health Food Debate

There's one thing *all* lesbians like to eat and though you'll probably feel quite satisfied after you've eaten it, it really doesn't have much nutritional value. This is where the consensus ends. When it comes to *real* food, tastes differ widely, dividing lesbians into two well-established and irreconcilable groups: Health Food Lesbians and Junk Food Lesbians. These two groups seem to fall along roughly the same lines as the Chemically Sensitive Lesbians and the Beer Drinking/Chain Smoking Lesbians. Below are some other common distinctions:

Health Food Lesbian

Works at the local food coop so that she can afford the 100 percent organic veggies and whole grain products that she cooks at home to ensure their nutrient integrity.

Slow eater because she eats a lot of raw, unruly, green things that require a lot of chewing.

Often says things like "Good Lord! Get that hamburger away from me. I can feel the spirit of the cow in the room and it's weeping!"

Grows sprouts in her closet.

Has no sex drive because of a B$_{12}$ deficiency.

Thinks cookies are better with brown rice syrup.

Her motto is "If it tastes good, spit it out."

Thinks a Twinkie is a diminutive lesbian.

Will abstain from eating food that might have just one verboten ingredient.

Junk Food Lesbian

Eats at the ballpark because she "likes the food."

Fast eater because she chooses foods (microwave burritos, Pop Tarts, etc.) that are so processed they are practically predigested.

Often says things like "I'll have the Big Mac Value Meal, please."

Has mold growing in the vegetable crisper of her fridge.

Likes to follow sex with Haägen-Dazs.

Thinks cookies are better with Crisco.

Her motto is "If it tastes like cardboard, spit it out."

Thinks Morning Thunder tea is a laxative.

Will simply push the mushrooms over to the side of her plate.

Will spend hours chopping, grating, mincing, and dicing so that everything is fresh.	Likes to boil her dinner in a bag.
Treats herself to a Rice Dream banana split once in a blue moon.	Thinks Baskin-Robbins is a restaurant.
Smells like garlic.	Smells like Doritos.
Talks constantly about "food combining."	Talks constantly about eating Combos.

Lesbians from the old school claim that the goddess made the distinction between Junk Food and Health Food Lesbians for a reason. They say that we can try to respect the values and customs of those who eat differently from us, but we should never mingle too closely because of the very real risk of intermarriage. These older lesbians claim that when the strict vegan falls in love with the carnivore whose favorite foods are Slim Jims and pork rinds, rancor and irreconcilable differences are the inevitable result.

Younger lesbians often rebel against labels altogether. They say things like "It's the individual food, not the food category—I just enjoy *food*. Sometimes I like organic broccoli and sometimes I like a Diet Coke. Get off my case."

Many experts now believe that these labels are really too rigid; that, in fact, Health Food Lesbians and Junk Food Lesbians are really the extreme poles on a spectrum of food preference. They claim that most people fall somewhere nearer to the middle, enjoying foods like hamburger nori rolls.

The Five Lesbian Brothers recommend a nondogmatic approach to food. We recognize that the different stages of your lesbian life have different nutritional requirements.

Cycle I

For those just coming out, we recommend macaroni and cheese, chocolate milkshakes, hot open-faced turkey sandwiches—you know, comfort food; the kind of food your mother would serve you if she was still speaking to you.

Cycle II

For newly in-love lesbians, we advise an IV hookup that can provide basic nutrients without interrupting sex.

Cycle III

For lesbians in long-term relationships suffering from lesbian bed death, we suggest heart-healthy, low-fat recipes such as tofu stir-fry and steamed veggies, since women in this category substitute food for sex and generally eat about twelve or thirteen meals a day.

"What Becomes a Lesbian Most": Dykes and Fashion
Time Line of Lesbian Evolution

Lesbians did not just spring forth from the head of Zeus like the goddess Athena! We evolved! In tracing the evolution of the lesbian, it becomes clear that lesbians have been fashion trendsetters since the first humans walked the earth (upright).

Homo erectus
(Pleistocene)

Lesbo erectus *(Tribadis numero-unus,* Pleistocene Era). Reason dictates that lesbians evolved from primates just like everyone else (with the possible exception of creationists). It is undisputed fact that at least one of the first humans was a lesbian, since this is when tools were first invented. These prehistoric lesbians walked around naked, even at this early stage refusing to wear the inhumane furs of their contemporaries. (NOTE: Many lesbians continue to sport the hairy legs of our ancestors.)

Amazon Warrior
2000 Years B.C.

Amazon Warriors *(Mono-mammalia aggressivus,* 2000 B.C.).
The Amazons were a feared and respected tribe of women warriors, long before the Lesbian Avengers. The single-breasted
doublet worn by the Amazon was copied by Grace Jones for
her *Nightclubbing* album, which in turn began a whole new
trend for S/M enthusiasts.

Witches
(1300–1500)

Witches *(Glinda persecutus,* 1300–1500). Jeanne d'Arc is probably the most famous witch of all times. She was burned at the stake for being a heretic, and not dressing according to her sex. The trial record reflects that Jeanne appeared before her tribunal dressed in "a grey tunic, a knee length cloak, black hose and a pair of boots." Fortunately, these crimes are no longer punishable by death or there would be no lesbians left in the East Village. The next time you lace up your Doc Martens, bow your head and give thanks.

Virgins/Whores
(1600–1872)

Virgins/Whores *(Hymen intacticus/Legus spreadicus,* 1600–1872). In Shakespeare's era, women who did not want to marry had two choices: the nunnery or the brothel. Going to Smith College simply wasn't an option back then. Since neither of these options is very appealing, we assume the majority of the nonmarrying types were sexual outlaws looking for a place to stay. It is these women who paved the way for the current crop of independent women of today who embody both archetypes at the same time: e.g., Madonna (Ciccone).

Spinsters
(1860s–1930s)

Spinsters *(Prunus autonomus,* 1860s–1930s). "Dowdy" probably best describes the style of the spinster who dressed in
layer upon layer of dull-colored clothing that hid her womanly
figure; she wore her hair either pulled back into a severe bun
or completely unkempt. We believe these women must have
heard the very same protestations we hear from our mothers to
this very day: "Why do you have to dress to make yourself as
unattractive to men as possible!?" Today it is called dressing
down and this time-honored lesbian tradition still works.

Lesbian Feminists
(1969–1979)

Lesbian Feminists *(Platex infernicus,* 1969–1979). Lesbian feminists cavorted braless through the sixties and seventies, being the first women to go without mammary restraints since a lesbian first invented the wheel, proving true the old fashion adage "Just wait, it will come back!"

Sex Artists
(1980s–present)

Sex Artists *(Bumpus publicus,* 1980s–present). Formerly whores, then elevated to ladies of the evening, lesbian sex artists are modern-day gurus who have literally raised the practice of sex to an art. These women choose poetry, visual arts, theater, and film to express themselves; funding their work through grants and the occasional sale of "dirty" underwear through the mail. These women are gifted at sex and are clearly the pinnacle of lesbian evolution.

Ice-Pick-Wielding Lesbian
Mankillers
(October 1992-November 1993)

Ice-Pick-Wielding Lesbian Mankillers *(Vaginus dentatus,* six months in 1992). Though short-lived, you can instantly recognize the ice-pick-wielding lesbian killer of the early 1990s because her tight skirts require that she never wear underwear. This fashion isn't new; it was invented by Raquel Welch in *One Million Years B.C.*

Supermodels
(1991–present)

Supermodels *(Clotheshorse neuroticus,* 1991–present). Though lesbian supermodels are few in number, their influence is enormous—not because they affect how lesbians dress, but because they make lesbianism seem fashionable. Our supermodel sisters don't put on and take off their sexuality the way they do their expensive clothes. No, these ladies wear their lesbianism all year round, regardless of the fashion, putting the style in our lifestyle.

Lesbian Moms
(Present)

Lesbian Moms (*Familiasvalue expandicus,* present). Lesbian moms are one of the few types of lesbians that accessorize. Look closely, you will never see a lesbian mom without a Snugli, a Binky, a cooler full of snacks for the kiddies, and a copy of *Heather Has Two Mommies* and *What If Your Child Is Straight.* This woman is a trendsetter for the future.

"Our Bodies/Our Hair"

Body hair is perhaps the hottest topic facing the lesbian community today. In our research for this book, everyone we talked to had something to say about body hair. How about you? Do you like a little or a lot? Here's your chance to create your perfect body hair fantasy girl.

Unlike most women, hair on the head is completely optional.

Hairy armpits: Is she gay or just European?

Hairy chest: A little hereditary gift from grandma?

All dykes have nipple hair.

Does she bleach, or wear her mustache proudly?

A few stray hairs or a full goatee?

Treasure trail.

Hobbit feet?

Busch Gardens or Mt. Baldy?

The legs: To shave or not to shave?

PART VII

ARTS AND ENTERTAINMENT

The Brothers have scanned the world of popular culture up, down, back, and forth, and what follows are a few of the highlights:

Best in Movies:
The Brothers' Night Out

Most Silicon-Implanted Portrayal of a Lesbian:
Showgirls

Best Sexy French Movie:
Entre Nous

Best Lesbian "Horror" Movie:
The Killing of Sister George

Best First-Date Movie:
Go Fish

Best Date Movie When You're Already In Love:
Fried Green Tomatoes

Best Movie to Inspire Vegetarianism:
Babe

Best Movie to Take That Married Woman You're Working on To:
Desert Hearts

Hottest Sex Scene:
Gina Gershon and Jennifer Tilly in *Bound*

Best Movie to Make You Glad You Didn't Live in the Fifties:
The Children's Hour

Best Movie to Feed the Man-Hater in You:
A Question of Silence

Best Movies to See Women with Big Muscles:
Aliens, Pumping Iron II, Terminator 2

Kleenex Travel Pack Award:
Little Women (1994 version)

Most Talented Action Figure:
Tank Girl

Best Movie to Make a Trip to the Concession Counter During:
Three of Hearts

Movie That Is So Bad You Can't Make a Trip to the Concession
Counter 'Cause You're Having Too Much Fun Making Fun of It:
Nell

Best Portrayal of a Lesbian Ever:
Queen Latifah in *Set It Off*

Best Movie to Make You Feel Like Packin' a .45:
Thelma and Louise

Best in Music:
The Brothers' CD Changer

Best Commitment Ceremony Theme Song:
"Willow," Joan Armatrading

Best Lesbian "Blow Off" Song:
"You're Too Possessive," Joan Jett

Most Politically Correct Song:
Anything by Holly Near

Best Album to Obsess About Unavailable Women To:
Ingenue, k.d. lang

Most Depressing Breakup Song:
"Ain't Life a Brook," Ferron

Best Music to Set the Mood:
Billie Holiday

Best Album to Drive To:
Brave and Crazy, Melissa Etheridge

Best Portrayal of Jesus by a Lesbian:
Amy Ray of The Indigo Girls

Best Music to Help You Keep the Faith:
Sweet Honey in the Rock

Best Music to Surf By:
"Goofyfoot," Phranc

Best Music to Get a Tattoo By:
Tribe 8

Best Lesbian Anthem:
"The Queer Song," Two Nice Girls

Best of Television:
The Brothers' Comfy Sofa

Most Subliminal Homosexuality:
Cagney & Lacey

Best Butch Character:
Sally Solomon, *Third Rock from the Sun*

Best Show for Learning How to Dress at Work:
Murphy Brown

Funniest Real-Life Lesbian to Appear on *Matlock:*
Lea Delaria

Best Lesbian Cartoon Character:
Velma, *Scooby Doo*

Game Show Personality Most Likely to Be a Lesbian:
Fannie Flagg

Stupidest Furor over Lesbian Content:
The kiss between Roseanne and Mariel Hemingway

Cutest Straight Girl We Wish Was a Lesbian:
Jackie on *Roseanne*

Most Subtle Portrayal of a Lesbian by a Straight Woman:
Glenn Close as Grethe Cammermeyer in *Serving in Silence*

Best TV to Watch with a Group of Dykes:
Women's NCAA Final Four

Best Feminist Character on TV
Lisa Simpson, *The Simpsons*

Best Books:
The Brothers' Nightstand

Best Book When You Can't Get No Satisfaction:
Sex for One, by Betty Dodson

Best Read-Aloud Bedtime Book:
The Case of the Not-So-Nice Nurse, by Mabel Maney

Best Books to Give to Your Baby-Dyke Niece:
Harriet the Spy, To Kill a Mockingbird

Best Book to Get Everyone to Leave Your Vicinity on a Crowded
Bus:
The SCUM Manifesto, by Valerie Solanas

Best Book for Attracting Chicks in Public:
Susie Sexpert's Lesbian Sex World, by Susie Bright

Best Book About Sex Toys:
Good Vibrations: The Complete Guide to Vibrators, by Joani
Blank

Best Lesbian-Cat Relationship:
Chicken and Hothead, *Hothead Paisan: Homicidal Lesbian
Terrorist,* by Diane DiMassa

Best Book for Learning to Dismantle the Patriarchy:
Sister Outsider, by Audre Lorde

Best Book to Read When Your Girlfriend Tells You She's Going
Shopping but Is Really Having an Affair:
After Delores, by Sarah Schulman

Worst Book to Read When You're Thinking About Coming Out:
The Well of Loneliness, by Radclyffe Hall

Best Shame-Based Erotica:
Anything by Ann Bannon

Best Book to Have on Your Shelf to Let Everyone Know:
"Rubyfruit Jungle," by Rita Mae Brown

The Lesbian Gaze:
The Five Lesbian Brothers' Guide to Constructive Moviegoing, TV Watching, Book Reading, and Musical Enjoyment

The Movies

esbians love the movies. That's why the Five Lesbian Brothers have perfected the art of finding lesbian imagery even when there is none. As you will see from the following reviews, we have trained ourselves to look for embedded lesbian allusions and subplots imperceptible to the untrained eye. We rate the movies on a five-finger rating system. Our highest rating is "The Golden Fist" for the movie onto which we can project the most lesbian content. Take a few moments to learn our method of watching movies and your next cinema experience will be much more dyke-positive, we guarantee it!

King Kong: The Remake. King Kong is a clear metaphor for lesbian love. The totally foxy Fay Wray character, played in the remake by Jessica Lange (over forty and still no facial surgery—go, Jess!), is loved in an awkward and somewhat dysfunctional way by the giant gorilla. Kong clearly represents the big, slightly too hairy butch girl whom society abhors, but who, nonetheless, is capable of great feeling. This touching lesbian love story is set at the Empire State Building and is clearly the inspiration for *Sleepless in Seattle*. We liked it and we give it three big, hairy, lesbian fingers.

Point Break. If you picture Keanu Reeves and Patrick Swayze as two lesbians (easy), you will realize this is a movie about lesbians who are too afraid to have sex with each other, so they just keep playing sports together. Reeves and Swayze have real chemistry as the romantic leads and Lori Petty (a REAL babe) makes this the perfect lesbian triangle movie. Watch carefully for the scene where Johnny Utah (Keanu) tells Bodhi (Patrick), "You gotta go down!" Also, when renting, hit pause as soon as Lori Petty runs out of the room after shooting at Keanu; nice butt, Lori. This movie gets a Golden Fist: All the Way to the Wrist.

Fried Green Tomatoes. This movie is initially very confusing. It seems like the two women really are in love with each other, although it is sometimes hard to tell what they are saying with their "southern" accents. They do swim half-naked together, one dips her fingers into the other's honey jar, one dresses as a man in a community play, and they then have a sexy food fight. We kept waiting for them to kiss, but they never did. The dead giveaway that this is a lesbian film is that the femme dies tragically and the butch is very sad. This is a three-finger movie— even though there's no explicit sex, it makes you mentally picture yourself having explicit sex with either Mary Stuart

Masterson or Mary-Louise Parker (depending on if you are a femme or a butch).

The Turning Point. Shirley MacLaine established her credentials as a screen lesbian, and established them big, early in her career with *The Children's Hour.* But in this movie, instead of being all clingy and co-dependent and going off and hanging herself over her girlfriend, this time she gets to have a good old-fashioned dyke brawl with her girl. The sexual energy between Anne Bancroft and Shirley MacLaine was terrific. Although we never actually saw them making out, we did get to see them pull each other's hair, and so we can imagine the rest. We enjoyed the shot of Mikhail Barishnikov's butt, but we felt there was not a sordid-enough portrait of the dance world. We wanted more drugs and starvation and more sex between ballerinas. We give this movie four fingers.

Thelma and Louise. Lesbians really liked this movie and we can see why. People think lesbians are just women who want to have sex with each other, but really we are women who want to have sex with each other and blow guys away or just blow up their stuff. This movie is the perfect embodiment of the famous Ferron song where "the lines connect and the point stays free." Thelma and Louise are nothing if not autonomous by the end of this flick. This is a four-finger movie. We would have given this movie a Golden Fist if they would have kissed longer at the end, maybe with a little tongue.

The Ten Commandments. The best scene in this movie is where everyone is worshiping the Golden Calf. You get the feeling people are having a good time; sort of like Gay Pride. We also really enjoyed Anne Baxter's carnal appetite, but

Moses is boring and lives by too many rules. He ends up wrecking all the fun—even though he himself has just been talking to a "burning bush"! Wake up, Moses! Take two tablets and leave our people alone until morning. We liked the movie a lot better than the book. We give it two fingers.

Friday the 13th. This movie blends really great horror with hockey. What could be better? We really like that heterosexual teenagers are slaughtered when they consummate their relationships. We think Jason must be some pissed-off lesbian who wreaks her revenge on all those smarmy "rights of passage" movies about boys. We give it two bloody fingers.

The Blob. We liked the female erotic qualities of the main character: red, formless, undulating, quivering, pulsing, throbbing. The Blob was not in nearly enough scenes and was treated as a menacing creature by all the men who just wanted to destroy it somehow. If some female character would have been put on the case, perhaps they would have made friends with The Blob and then had sex with each other. That would have made this movie better. This movie gets a Golden Fist because, even though the main female characters don't have sex with each other, on a political level, it doesn't pull any punches when it comes to vagina envy.

Terminator 2. This movie was completely unrealistic. We found it very hard to believe that Linda Hamilton could be running around in that tank top and those boots, escaping from mental hospitals, shooting high-powered rifles, lobbing hand grenades, and saving the world in general and still not have a girlfriend! It just didn't make any sense. We're saving our fingers for Linda in the sequel.

Lesbian TV Guide

Think of all the hours you spent watching TV as an unhappy, maladjusted prehomosexual youth. Now consider them again, using our high-powered homoscope. The more you utilize our methods the more you will realize that television is swarming with prime-time tribades.

6:30 P.M. (5) ROSEANNE Dan is threatened when Roseanne flirts with Darlene's girlfriend. (r) 8759

7:00 P.M. (5) HOME IMPROVEMENT *Tool Time* takes on a whole new meaning when Tim discovers a glory hole in Wilson's fence. (r) 93274

7:30 P.M. (5) THE SIMPSONS Lisa diligently practices for the battle of the saxophones despite accusations of lesbianism. (r) 3939

9:00 P.M. (2) MURPHY BROWN Murph gets into a tight spot when she fists Corky and is accused of sexual harassment. 856787

9:00 P.M. (F) X-FILES Scully falls under the spell of an eerie tennis star. (Part 1 of 2). 856787

10:00 P.M. (2) CHICAGO HOPE A crazed lesbian opens fire in the ER when she is denied spousal access. (CC) 337837

11:00 P.M. (5) COPS Lesbian cops infiltrate separatist encampment and give strong warning to members about firing at neighbors. (CC) 911911

11:30 P.M. (2) LATE SHOW WITH DAVID LETTERMAN Phranc, k.d. lang, Madonna, Rosie O'Donnell sing medley of Lennon Sisters Greatest Hits. Guest host Lily Tomlin. (CC) (11:35) 387429

4:30 A.M. (LIFE) MELROSE PLACE Kimberly develops another personality and begins hitting on all the girls! (r) 932473

Lesbian Gaze Quiz

Yₒu can get yourself all worked up into a lather about lesbian invisibility or you can just pretend everything is really about you. Have a little fun with your newfound skills with this quiz.

1. The most anticipated dyke movie of all time might have been:

   ❏ a. Eager Beavers (D. Clarence Brown)
   ❏ b. Eaten Alive (D. Tobe Hooper)
   ❏ c. Wild Strawberries (D. Ingmar Bergman)
   ❏ d. Salmonberries (D. Percy Adlon)

2. Which of the following is not a lesbian character?

   ❏ a. Jane Hathaway from the Beverly Hillbillies
   ❏ b. Buddy Lawrence from Family
   ❏ c. Leather Tuscadero from Happy Days
   ❏ d. Barney Fife from The Andy Griffith Show

3. You can be 100 percent absolutely sure that a character is a lesbian only when:

   ❏ a. She dies.
   ❏ b. She sucks another woman's blood.

❏ c. She kisses another woman on the mouth and uses her tongue.

❏ d. She kills a guy with an ice pick.

4. The most realistic portrayal of a lesbian in a movie would be:

❏ a. Amanda Donohoe in Lair of the White Worm

❏ b. Jane Alexander in Franklin and Eleanor

❏ c. Laurie Metcalf in Internal Affairs

❏ d. Jodie Foster in Sommersby

5. Which of the following would not qualify as a classic butch performance:

❏ a. Greta Garbo in Queen Christina

❏ b. Mercedes McCambridge in Johnny Guitar

❏ c. Katharine Hepburn in Sylvia Scarlett

❏ d. John Hurt in The Naked Civil Servant

6. Worst case of celluloid lesbian Kissus interruptus:

❏ a. Demi Moore and Whoopi Goldberg in Ghost

❏ b. Jodie Foster and Nastassja Kinski in The Hotel New Hampshire

❏ c. Cagney and Lacey every time they go into the bathroom

7. Best movie about a lesbian who shoots a gun:

❏ a. The Man Who Shot Liberty Valance

❏ b. They Shoot Horses, Don't They?

❏ c. The Shootist

❏ d. I Shot Andy Warhol

8. Best lesbian movie ever written and/or directed by a man:

   ❏ a. Personal Hygiene
   ❏ b. Personal Best
   ❏ c. Personal Breast
   ❏ d. Personnel Test

9. The girl least likely to be a lesbian:

   ❏ a. Jo in Little Women
   ❏ b. Jo on The Facts of Life
   ❏ c. Jo in The Ballad of Little Jo
   ❏ d. Bobbie Jo on Petticoat Junction

10. The hottest lesbian kiss in any movie:

   ❏ a. Jennifer Tilly and Gina Gershon in Bound
   ❏ b. Glenn Close and Judy Davis in Serving in Silence: The Grethe Cammermeyer Story
   ❏ c. Jodie Foster and Richard Gere in Sommersby
   ❏ d. Jack Lemmon and Tony Curtis in Some Like It Hot

The *New York Times* Bestseller List
(According to the Five Lesbian Brothers)

1. **WOMEN ARE FROM VENUS/MEN HAVE A PENIS**
   Communication between the sexes—who needs it?

2. **THE DYKES OF MADISON COUNTY**
   Girl saves the residents of Madison County by sticking her finger in a local dyke.

3. **THE ROAD EVEN LESS TRAVELED THAN THE ROAD LESS TRAVELED**
   Spiritual teachings for social outcasts.

4. **LESBIAN BE NOT PROUD**
   Surviving in the closet.

5. **IT TAKES THE VILLAGE PEOPLE**
   Inspiring story of children raised by drag queens.

6. **I'M OKAY, YOU'RE A LESBIAN**
   Phyllis Schlafly speaks her mind.

7. **LESBIANS FOR DUMMIES**
   Beginner's guide to the world's most popular lifestyle.

8. **DYKANETICS**
   Reveals what the "L" in "L. Ron Hubbard" really stands for.

9. **MY HOT ZONE**
   Steamy story of two girls' discovery in the jungle.

10. **FOR WHOM THE FEMME TOLLS**
    Story of a lesbian who attempts to overthrow the patriarchy by allowing lesbians to exit New Jersey Turnpike for free.

Fun Songs to Sing at the Revolution,
or New Lyrics for Old Standards

Imagine what your childhood would have been like if your family had sung songs like *these* on long car trips.

Sung to the tune of "Our Love Is Here to Stay":
It's very queer. Our love is here to stay
Look in the mirror/face the fact you're gay

Sung to the tune of "She'll Be Comin' Round the Mountain":
She'll be coming and I'll mount her when she comes
She'll be coming and I'll mount her when she comes
She'll be coming and I'll mount her
With my legs all wrapped around her
She'll be coming and I'll mount her when she comes.

Sung to the tune of "My Darling Clementine":
She is darling, she is darling, she is darling and she's mine
Thought I'd lost her to a straight guy but she's back for the third time.

Sung to the tune of "Camptown Ladies":
P-Town Lezzies sing this song—Dildo, dildo
Like to ride that latex dong
All the Dildo Day.

Sung to the tune of "I've Been Working on the Railroad":
I've been working on my girlfriend

All the livelong day
I've been working on my girlfriend
I sure hope that she is gay.

Sung to the tune of "Home on the Range":
Ho-mo on the range
Where that queer and my aunt eloped. Yea!

Sung to the tune of "This Land Is Your Land":
This land is your land, this land is my land
Oh no, there's a man on the land
Cover your tits with your hands.

Sung to the tune of "I Left My Heart in San Francisco":
I left my vibrator . . . in San Francisco.

PART VIII

THE LEISURELY LESBIAN (GAMES, SPORTS, TRAVEL)

Games for Girls
Who Like to Play with Other Girls

Welcome to the activity and puzzle pages of the book! These games were specially developed at the renowned Five Lesbian Brothers Laboratories to nurture the neglected lesbian child in you—that little baby muffdiver who was given Barbie and Ken when she really wanted Barbie and her butch girlfriend Midge, and was forced to play soul-killing games like Mystery Date. We, as lesbians, know that a real Mystery Date is telling your parents you're going to the mall when you're really going to make out with your girlfriend behind the sewage treatment facility. Now you can reclaim your lost youth with these special fun projects created just for you.

Connect the Dots

International symbol of pride
(When finished, fill in with pink marker.)

1,4 •   • 3

•
z

Recognize anyone?

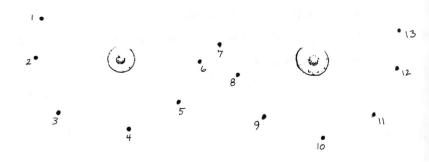

You can find this on your pillowcase or on a can of Coke.

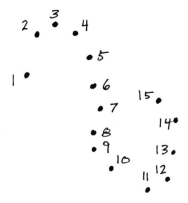

Ancient Amazon warrior symbol.

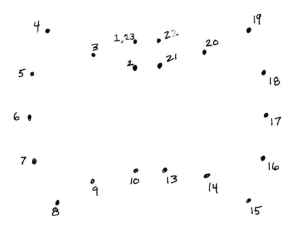

Who's passed out at the bar?

Where's Dildo?

H i, there, Dildo watchers. I'm slippery and slimy and fit just about anywhere. (Don't forget the lube!) Can you find me in the sea of lesbians with fuzzy knit caps?

Lesbian Word Search

```
R  S  L  B  N  R  Q  D  I  L  D  O  W  P  C  S  Y
T  O  M  A  N  H  A  T  E  R  B  C  G  J  L  K  K
M  N  S  P  E  R  M  D  O  N  O  R  K  Y  O  Z  O
F  H  T  S  C  V  D  G  B  U  T  C  H  N  S  Y  C
S  C  R  L  W  F  T  B  A  E  C  A  T  O  E  R  L
M  D  A  M  N  L  S  P  Q  X  D  T  L  A  T  K  J
V  R  P  A  R  I  A  H  C  P  T  Z  M  K  C  W  I
S  S  O  C  I  A  L  W  O  R  K  E  R  B  A  O  A
T  U  N  W  N  J  M  K  L  R  O  A  R  N  S  M  E
S  P  H  G  S  L  O  E  I  H  T  W  Y  X  E  O  N
S  T  S  A  E  Z  N  B  V  C  D  M  O  K  J  N  L
K  J  F  E  M  R  B  S  I  U  Y  T  V  C  L  P  A
N  J  T  A  I  K  E  O  A  W  I  M  M  I  N  N  G
S  M  Y  T  N  U  R  W  C  K  N  E  C  D  K  J  G
D  K  T  X  A  W  R  Y  R  Z  B  A  F  L  M  O  T
K  J  C  X  T  Z  I  X  U  Y  W  E  O  I  U  T  X
K  B  J  D  E  L  E  M  I  T  M  R  U  N  M  W  O
S  T  R  N  Y  P  S  T  S  M  J  K  L  M  T  W  A
P  T  C  D  R  H  T  Z  E  Q  N  S  T  R  T  W  A
```

Find the following:
butch, femme, dildo, closetcase, manhater, spermdonor, oliviacruise, strapon, salmonberries, wymyn, womon, wimmin, socialworker, inseminate, pariah

Link

E ver slept with Martina? Bet you're closer than you think. Just fill in the blanks and once and for all establish your sexual connection with the lesbian of your dreams.

I_____slept with_____who slept with_____who slept with_____who slept with Martina.

See? Try this one:
I_____slept with_____who slept with_____who slept with_____who slept with Madonna.

Or what about this:
I_____slept with_____who slept with_____who slept with_____who slept with Melissa Etheridge.

Advanced version: Identify the "HUBS." As you play this game with your friends, you'll realize that some women are HUBS. They've slept with everyone! If *you* sleep with a HUB, you can get to almost *anyone* in TWO STEPS!

Sodomy Map

odomy Map is a fun game you can play with a single partner or with any number of partners. Simply buy yourself a map of the United States. Use a pink highlighter to color in the states that have obsolete sodomy laws still on the books. Whenever you are in one of those states, be sure to have a sexual experience that involves cunnilingus, anal penetration, and fisting. CONGRATULA-TIONS! You boinked a girl in Georgia! Now you can mark that state with a pushpin! Keep going until you collect all twenty-two states.

State-by-State "Sodomy" Laws

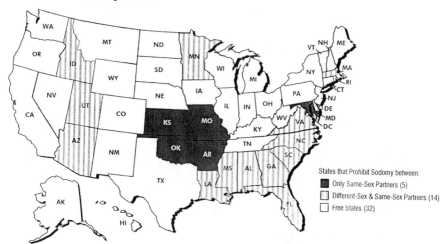

States that Prohibit Sodomy between:

- ■ Only Same-Sex Partners (5)
- ▨ Different-Sex & Same-Sex Partners (14)
- □ Free States (32)

Supreme Court Test Case

Supreme Court Test Case is a simple game you can play that usually involves at least two players but can go into the hundreds.

First: **CHOOSE A SITE.** Choosing the right site is important. You want to be someplace where you will really offend and upset people to the point where they will take you all the way to the Supreme Court to challenge your right to do whatever "action" it is you chose to do. A few good suggestions are:

Hotel swimming pools in the Bible Belt
Houses of worship
"Mixer" events on U.S. military installations
Senate floor
Elementary school playgrounds
Cracker Barrel restaurants

Second: **CHOOSE THE RIGHT CLOTHES.** The important thing about dressing up for Supreme Court Test Case is that somehow you must make it very clear that you are BOTH WOMEN. Leave nothing to the breeders' imaginations because, unless you take precautions, they will see what they want to see: a young man and woman making out. Remember, for every *three* "male indicators" it takes for someone to identify you as "male," there are *twelve* "female indicators" necessary for you to be identified as a female. So *think about it.*

Third: **TAKE ACTION.** We recommend kissing and light fondling on top of the clothes. Remember, this is a game of SUPREME COURT TEST CASE! You are not playing Sodomy Map (see Sodomy Map above). Actively make out and fondle until you are arrested or thrown out.

Fourth: **CALL LAMBDA LEGAL DEFENSE AND EDUCATION FUND.**

Fifth: **TAKE YOUR CASE ALL THE WAY TO THE SUPREME COURT.**

Variations for Advanced Players:

- Adopt a kid in California.
- Get hitched in Hawaii.
- Tell without being asked.

Know Your Lesbian Rumors

Don't you hate it when you say to your straight friend, "Barbara Stanwyck was a lesbian," and they say, "How do you know?" and, though you know for sure it is true, all you can say is, "She just is." And don't you hate it even more when you get all excited because you hear that someone you absolutely adore, like Holly Hunter, is a lesbian, and you go around blabbing it to anyone who cares to listen and then you find out later she's happily married to a man? Let's face it! Rumors are all we have until they perfect that chemical in vaginal secretions that makes your tongue turn blue.

Which one of the following rumors would you be most likely to repeat at a party?

a. Whitney Houston punched out Jodie Foster when she caught her making love to Kelly McGillis on the set of *The Accused.*
b. The father of Whitney Houston's child is *not* Bobby Brown, but rather the brother of Whitney's longtime lesbian companion, "Robyn."
c. The "Captain" in Captain and Tenille used to be a woman.

a. Rosie O'Donnell is a muffdiver.
b. Cindy Crawford is a muffdiver.
c. Kathie Lee Gifford is a muffdiver.

a. Janet Reno wears slippers at the Justice Department.
b. Janet Reno smokes a pipe.
c. Janet Reno likes to be addressed as "Mister Reno."

a. Julie Andrews and Blake Edwards have a bearded marriage.
b. Joanne Woodward and Paul Newman have a bearded marriage.
c. Santa Claus and Pavarotti are married and have beards.

a. Jodie Foster was lovers with Helen Hunt.
b. Jodie Foster was lovers with Linda Hunt.
c. Jodie Foster was lovers with the cast of *Hunter.*

The Sports Page

Not all female athletes are lesbians and not all lesbians are athletes. Still, it is true that many of us found our way to self-acceptance and pride on the playing field in the company of other sweaty women. Whether we participate in sports because we want to crush our opponents or simply because we have a crush on one of our opponents doesn't matter. It's not whether we win or lose, it's whom we get to go home with after the game. For many of us, the heat of competition generates another kind of heat. And so we analyzed our top eleven favorite sports to see which sport makes the best foreplay.

Sport	Physical Contact	Setting	Outfit
SOFTBALL	Butt pats, sliding, celebratory pileup	Neighborhood diamond	Polyester uniform with bar sponsor name
BASKETBALL	A lot for a non-contact sport	Forgiving wood or punishing concrete	Flimsy tank top, gigantic shorts
BOWLING	When some prankster grabs your ball from behind	Cavernous alley on the outskirts of town, often near a Red Lion Inn	Short-sleeved, button-down shirt with your name embroidered over the breast pocket
RUGBY	Constant (scrum). Sudden and violent (back line)	Big green field, rain, shine, or blizzard	Heavy shirt with rubber buttons, tiny shorts, jog bra, cup
FIELD HOCKEY	Severe	Prep school	Lesbian classic: skirt and tie
TENNIS	Sweaty-palmed handshake at the end	Wimbledon	Cute little white girlie things

Personality Type	Equipment	How to Win	Injury/Risks
Jolly	Bat, ball, mitt, cooler	Hit, steal, and run home	Torn rotator cuff, catcher's knee, bee stings
Lanky and mellow (center). Compact and intense (guard)	Ball, basket, elbows	Flubber	Concussion, stress fracture, splinters in butt
Working gal	Balls, pins, little pencils	Use a clean eraser	Wrist sprain, smashed windshield in parking lot
Borderline	Cleats, ball, beer ball	Penetration, penetration, penetration	Dislocated knee, black eye, brain damage
Cruel and arbitrarily violent	Sticks, balls, shin guards	Distract goalie by lifting your skirt	Bloody shins
Autonomous, likes to keep to her side of the bed	Racquet, balls, ball girls	You must understand that love means nothing	Tennis elbow, palimony suits, stab wounds

Sport	Physical Contact	Setting	Outfit
SWIMMING	No actual physical contact but plenty of opportunity to ogle	Pool	The minimum allowed by law
SURFING	To be avoided at all times, no dings	Ocean	Wetsuit
GOLF	Incidental butt brush in the heavy crowds at the Dinah Shore Classic	Undulating natural surface with eighteen holes	Cleats, shorts with a crease, snappy visor
BILLIARDS	Occasional drunken brawl when someone takes your quarter	Smoky bars and pool halls, parents' basement	Jeans, boots, tight tank top
DARTS	Sitting on girlfriend's lap between turns	Bar at happy hour	What you wore to work

Personality Type	Equipment	How to Win	Injury/Risks
Slippery when wet	Goggles, cap, steroids	Nair	Strained shoulder, crappy dried-out hair, red eyes, drowning, shot by accident with starter pistol
Zen	Board, nose coat	King Neptune lets you live	Shark attack, drowning, losing all ambition to get a real job
Peppy, possible Scottish ancestry	Clubs, balls, foxy young caddy	Sensitive stroke	Strained shoulder, inability to escape sand trap
Chemically dependent	Ten balls and a big stick, high alcohol tolerance	Know all the angles	Getting poked in the eye with cue, liver failure
Grandiose	Round board, three darts, supple wrist	Hit the bull's-eye (if you can still see it)	Dart holes in butt

Equipment is considered one of the highlights in any sport. When we had women select their favorite sport on the basis of equipment alone, this was the result:

1. Skydiving
2. Rodeo
3. Stock car racing
4. Climbing
5. Cycling
6. Dog sledding
7. American Gladiators
8. Luge
9. Football
10. Scuba diving

Favorite deodorant of lesbian athletes:

1. Secret
2. Tickle
3. Old Spice
4. Rock crystal
5. Lemon juice
6. What's wrong with the way I smell?

Top Ten Lesbian Sports Heroines

1 . MARTINA

Martina is *número uno* because she was the first really famous female athlete to come out as a lesbian. That's what most lesbians will say. The real reason she is *número uno* is because we all like to picture ourselves trapped in the steel grip of her thighs.

2. MONICA SELES

Monica is not a lesbian (or, if she is, she isn't out), but lesbians identify with Monica because she was stabbed in the back. She is also a sexy combination of superpower/underdog. *"Ai-eee!"*

3. FLO-JO

Florence Griffith-Joyner is not a lesbian. We can tell by looking at those nails. But she is fast.

4. DIANA NYAD

Lesbians love all swimmers because swimming is about the sexiest sport in the world since it involves submerging oneself in fluid. (It's nice to have a girlfriend who can hold her breath for two minutes at a time.) Our favorite swimmers are the ones who stay in the water for forty-eight hours at a time, braving everything from ocean swells to sharks to hypothermia. We see distance swimming as a metaphor for our lives. Is Diana an out lesbian? (Where's our researcher?)

5. BABE DIDRIKSON

Babe is dead but her memory lingers. Babe used to be number one with lesbians until Martina blew the field wide open. Babe was not a lesbian (at least that's what her husband said), but she did personify the lesbian dream of being a universal athlete. Interestingly, "Babe" is still the number-one nickname that young tomboys employ when choosing their sports identity.

6. SUSAN BUTCHER

Also known as "Dog Sled Lady," this incredible woman won the Iditarod eight times. She is not a lesbian, but she might as well be since she spends all her time with her animal companions.

7. PAULA NEWBY-FRASER

Paula has won the Gatorade Ironman Triathlon eight times. Lesbians really appreciate Paula because, even though she is a straight woman, Paula is not afraid to wear the label "Ironman."

8. BEV FRANCIS

Co-star of that lesbian favorite *Pumping Iron II: The Women,* this humpy Australian takes butch all the way with her vein-popping biceps. Bev must be a lesbian. She is a heroine to many of us because even though she succumbs to using some scary makeup, she remains all butch and powerful.

9. BLAZE

American Gladiator Extraordinaire. Juiced-up on steroids—but, hey, testosterone isn't just for men anymore! Many a dyke has braved the big tennis-ball-shooting gun just to be in the same room with this action figure of a woman. We know we don't like to miss our date with her every Saturday.

10. SECRETARIAT

Secretariat wasn't a lesbian—in fact, Secretariat was a horse and was not even female. He just had a deceptively female name, like Lassie. Lesbians relate to Secretariat, however, because he represents the lesbian dream of being put out to stud.

My Dinner with . . .

_____ was very_____
name of person in room   adjective

She was driving across the country in her new _____
                                                      name of vehicle

to meet _____ . She had entered the contest
          lesbian celebrity

held by her favorite brand of _____ tea and she had
                                        flavor

won a romantic dinner with _____.
                              repeat celebrity name

"_____!" she whispered as she entered the restaurant.
   exclamation

"I haven't been any place this _____ since I was
                                    adjective

dating _____!" Suddenly _____
          name of someone known to group   repeat celebrity

walked in. She looked _____. _____
                          adjective   repeat name of person in room

felt her mouth get all_____. She began to
                          adjective

_____ in her seat_____.
verb   adverb

"Is there something in your _____ or are you
                                body part

just happy to see me?" said _____.
                              repeat celebrity

"I'm sorry," said _____."You look so _____
                    repeat first name   adjective

You make me feel totally _____." "You're not so
                              adjective

_____ yourself," said _____.
adjective   celebrity

The dinner was _____. They ordered
adjective

_____ and_____ and
food item   food item

gazed into each other's _____while they ate
body part

_____. "Would you like to come to my _____?
adverb   noun

We could _____." "Oh, _____, I've
verb   repeat celebrity

never been so _____. I think I _____ you!"
adjective   verb

Festival Fun!

Once when _____ went to the _____
name of person in room   geographical location

Women's Music Festival, she _____ walked
adverb

into the tent of _____,who was_____.
lesbian celebrity   verb

Their _____s met and they knew it was
body part

only a matter of time until they _____ with
verb past tense

each other. Suddenly, _____'s _____
repeat first person   adjective

girlfriend _____stormed in. "You little _____!"
noun

name of person known to group

she _____. "You were supposed to meet me in the
verb past tense

_____tent at noon. We're breaking up and I'm
activity

taking the _____ with me! Oh, and tell your
             plural noun

little_____ her _____is show-
    noun   *body part*

ing and it's_____."
         adjective

Home for the Holidays

"Happy _____!" Mother _____
      name of holiday   *adverb*

exclaimed. Everyone at the table was very _____.
                                           emotion

Dad was on his _____ _____ and so he was
                   number   *alcoholic beverage*

feeling _____. I knew it was not the _____
      emotion   *adjective*

time to come out to them, but my _____
                                relation

Cindy had advised me that I should. My _____
                                             relation

Bill was _____ his face with his _____
             verb   *adjective*

mouth open, which distracted me. Finally, I said,

"_____, I have something to tell you.
  relation

I am a _____."
      noun

Where Have All the Lesbians Gone

(On Vacation)?

Yes, we are everywhere. But there are more of us in these four cities than anywhere else. So if you're looking to take a vacation to a place where no one will ask you the dreaded question, "Would you and your son like a room?," you might want to travel to one of these lesbian meccas.

San Francisco

If you're going to San Francisco, make sure to wear a big pink triangle on the lapel of your leather jacket. Then take the MUNI over to Castro Street and enjoy the friendly "vibe." There are so many gay people in San Fran you'll find yourself looking at straight people thinking, "What the hell are you doing here?" Sodom by the Sea, San Francisco lives up to its name. We estimate that this town has the most active dyke sex clubs and parties in all the fifty states. These adventuresome gals actually have public bondage and disciplinary sex. They don't just talk about it like the rest of us.

Provincetown

Every summer, lesbians flock to the tip of Cape Cod affectionately known as P-Town, where the light is exquisite and the landscape serene. But don't expect an introspective experience when you vacation in P-Town. The P stands for party, and, boy, can these girls show you how! Dykes drink here like it was 1952, and there is something about the sea breeze (or is it the Stingers?) that makes you forget that wedding ring on your finger. What better place to nurse a hangover than at Herring Cove, the world-famous "lesbian beach," where impetuous gals of all shapes, colors, sizes, and economic backgrounds are free to burn their exposed breasts. Make sure to listen for the "Ranger!" call or you may get a ticket along with your tan.

Northampton

Northampton has been identified by the *National Enquirer* as Dyketown USA, and we couldn't agree more. Conveniently located near several of the Seven Sister colleges, this quaint Connecticut River Valley town is a magnet for lesbians as well as women and men who appear to be lesbians. Apparently, the strong, self-respecting lady graduates are spoiled by the women-only atmosphere and are rendered unfit for life elsewhere. Here you will see lesbians stroll the streets, work at their jobs, raise their families, and just plain fit into the big picture as if there were some kind of lesbian "GI Bill." But be sure to take your American Express card because NoHo is not cheap and neither is your girlfriend.

New York

Park Slope, Brooklyn, and the East Village of Manhattan are both internationally renowned loci of lesbian vacation destinations. Both within the borders of the most exciting city since Gomorrah, these two neighborhoods offer distinctive entertainment and lifestyle choices for both the budding baby bulldagger and the sunset-years retirees alike. If you're under twenty-five and have a pierced septum, head for the East Village, where you can prowl the streets in search of dens that house others like you. For those of you seeking a more sedate New York experience, take the F train to Seventh Avenue in Brooklyn, where you can stroll down the "lesbian Champs-Elysées" and make eye contact with all the gorgeous gals in dreadlocks.

Even if you choose to travel to a "mainstream" attraction, your vacation can still have that special lesbian flavor.

Which well-known tourist attraction is more "lesbian"?

Mt. Rushmore or

Statue of Liberty

Sea World or

Disney

Mystery Spot or

Old Faithful

Grand Canyon or

Pike's Peak

Busch Gardens or

King's Dominion

Washington Monument

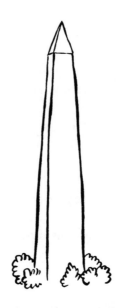

or Capitol Building

Closety Bar Names:
The Comprehensive List You've Been Waiting For

All homos-in-the-know know that when you're visiting a strange city and want to know where to find your tribe, you look for the gay and lesbo bar. Such establishments are always named to clue in us queers without alerting the natives. The following is a sample of *actual* bar names culled from the Gay Yellow Pages. (Seriously, we couldn't make this up if we tried!)

Bars with French Names

French Quarter, French Connections, Vieux Carré, Chez Est, Bon Mot, C'est La Guerre, La Fleur's, Déjà Vu, Chez Colette, C'est La Vie II

Bars Named After Feeling States

Sensations, Obsessions, Temptations, Expressions, Impressions, Inspirations, Reflections, Attitudes

States That Have Bars Named "Zippers"

Alabama, Georgia, Maryland, Michigan, South Carolina, Texas

States That Have Bars Named "Secrets"

Arizona, Maryland, Kentucky

States That Have Bars Named "Rumors" (or "Rumorz")

Arizona, California, New York, Ohio, Pennsylvania, Washington, Delaware, Maryland, Minnesota

States That Have Bars Named "Trax"

Arizona, South Carolina, California, Delaware, Florida, Georgia, Michigan, New York

Closety Names That Imply Hiding

Incognito Lounge, Winks, Incognito Valley, Shame on the Moon, Incognito Pasadena, Last Great Hiding Place, Alibi East, Hideaway, Grotto, Club Shadows, The Cove, Closet, Hideaway II, Hide-A-Way Club

Closety Names That Tell You Which Way to Enter

Back Door, Back Door Pub, Back Room, Backstreet, Hidden Door, Back Alley, Back Porch, Front Street, Down the Street, Across the Street

Sex Names

The Hole, The White Swallow (men), Ambush (women), Cheeks, Tight End, Bushwhackers, The Honey Pot, Bottoms Up, Vibrations (women), Different Strokes

The Coming-Out Names

Changes, Crossings, Discovery, Options, The Alternative, Contacts, The Other Side, The Lavender Door, Choices Pub,

New Beginnings, Chances, Bosom Buddies, Just Friends, The
Other Half

The Shame Names

Taboo, Secrets, Whispers, Street Talk, Promises, Scandals

Weird Names That We Like But Can't Figure Out

Mangos, The Parking Ramp, We Are Family, Jack's Con-
struction Site, Off Ramp Café, Spoiled Brat, Ginger's Tool

Gay Pop-Culture References

Marilyn's Closet, Emerald City, Oz, Over the Rainbow, La
Cage aux Folles, Victor/Victoria's, Toto's, Garbo's, Tootsie's,
Stage Door

Bar That Straight People Accidentally Walk Into

Oops

Birds or Bird Parts

Eagle, Raven, Lark, Falcon, Nitengale, Feathers, Wings,
Beaky's

The Lesbian Brain

Y ou won't find this in any science class, but you probably never studied Rita Mae Brown in high school English either.

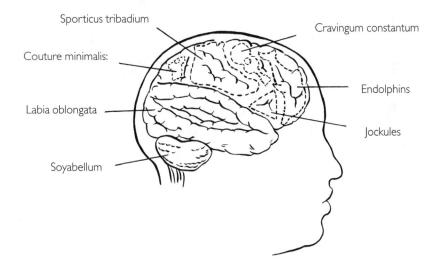

Labia oblongata: Largest portion of the brain, controlling the sex drive.

Endolphins: A hormone secreted by the labia oblongata that controls the desire for dolphin-shaped dildos.

Couture minimalis: The smallest section of the brain, governing fashion sense.

Sporticus tribadium: A portion of the brain that controls coordination.

Jockules: Little energy cells produced in the sporticus tribadium that enable you to jump higher and play longer.

Cravingum constantum: The part of the brain that is always playing a k.d. lang song.

Soyabellum: Controls love for tofu.

The Lesbian Creed

Remember, being a lesbian is a special gift. Treasure it and share it with as many people as possible. You can help yourself by starting and ending each day with this lesbian creed:

Please grant me the courage

to hold my girlfriend's hand

at family get-togethers,

the patience to keep my hands

off her in front of scary rednecks,

and the wisdom to tell

the difference.